Wendell was at his front d

"Now you boys be careful," his mother admonished. "I know how you are with your adventures, Josh."

She reached over and tried to kiss Wendell, but he shrugged away.

"Aw, Mom." He looked embarrassed.

"C'mon, Wendell," I said. "We're ready to go."

"I can't stand it when my mother gets mushy," said Wendell as we crossed the lawn.

As I pushed through my back door, I saw Sonny and my mom standing in front of each other holding hands. I hesitated. They moved together and Sonny kissed her lightly.

I turned quickly from the door and ran smack into Wendell, who was right behind me.

"What's wrong?" he said.

"I can't stand it when my mother gets mushy either," I said sharply. "Especially with somebody else."

Ask for these titles from Chariot Books

A JOSH McINTIRE BOOK

MURPHY'S MANSION

by Elaine K. McEwan

Chariot Books™
A Division of Cook Communications

Chariot Books™ is an imprint of David C. Cook Publishing Co.
David C. Cook Publishing Co., Elgin, Illinois 60120
David C. Cook Publishing Co., Weston, Ontario
Nova Distribution Ltd., Eastbourne, England

MURPHY'S MANSION
© 1994 by Elaine K. McEwan

Cover design by Elizabeth Thompson
Cover illustration by Robert Papp
First printing, 1994
Printed in the United States of America
98 97 96 95 94   5 4 3 2 1

Library of Congress Cataloging-in-Publication Data

McEwan, Elaine K.
      Murphy's mansion / Elaine K. McEwan.
                p.   cm.
      "A Josh McIntire book" —
      Summary: Between worrying about his mother's dates and dealing with
an unusual new girl in his sixth grade class, Josh tries to learn more about the
Murphy mansion and the old woman who lives there.
      ISBN 0-7814-0160-7
      [1. Schools—Fiction. 2. Christian life—Fiction. 3. Old age—Fiction. 4.
Divorce—Fiction.] I. Title.
PZ7.M4784545Mu   1994
[Fic]—dc20

                                                              94-7136
                                                                 CIP
                                                                  AC

To LuAnn Bombard,
Director, West Chicago City Museum
—Elaine K. McEwan

Special thanks to Mr. Brugmann's
sixth graders for their expert assistance
—LoraBeth Norton, Editor

I rode my bike aimlessly around the neighborhood. Mom wouldn't be home from work for another couple hours. My next door neighbor and best friend, Wendell, was away at camp. Even my grown-up friend Sonny didn't need me. His leather shop had been closed for most of the summer so he could tour with his band, The King's Messengers. Sonny was the drummer.

The humid, hazy August afternoon seemed endless. Perspiration trickled down my forehead, and I swatted the no-see-ums away as I rode.

I could clean my room, I thought. Mom had been bugging me since school was out to do that.

"You did a great job on toxic waste in Grandville," she had reminded me. "Now how about some action on that pile of garbage in your bedroom?"

I crossed that idea off my list. Too much work.

I thought of riding over to the library to see if they had any new books. I'd been reading a lot this summer. The best book so far was *Dear Mr. Henshaw*. It was about a kid whose parents were divorced, just like mine.

I remembered how last summer, when we first moved to Grandville, I thought Wendell was weird because he went to the library in the summertime. Boy, have I changed, and in more ways than one. I even look different. I've grown a couple of inches, and my hair is getting curlier.

I dismissed the library idea too.

Mom hates it when I say I'm bored, but she couldn't hear me, so I said it out loud. "I'm bored."

Nothing happened. The street was deserted. I said it again, louder this time. "I'm bored!"

A mangy black dog barked at me. He was tied to a porch railing and looked bored too. I watched him lap water from a dirty pail.

Suddenly I felt thirsty. I could ride to Coach's Corner Confectionery, the new ice cream place on Main Street. Now there was an idea worth pursuing. I checked my pockets and found just enough change for a small cone.

"Thanks!" I yelled at the dog. He'd given me a great idea.

He looked at me with soulful eyes and went back to drinking.

The route to Coach's was a familiar one. I had to pass my school and go through town.

Jefferson School looked like I felt . . . lonely. There were weeds growing up through the cracks in the asphalt. I'd be in sixth grade when school started. That was a promising thought. Sixth graders were top dogs at Jefferson.

While riding past the school I got a great idea. I'd take a detour. See the sights of Grandville. Discover Mystery, Romance, and Adventure on the way to Coach's Corner. As long as I was headed toward town, I knew I couldn't get lost.

My mother wouldn't have been happy if she could have read my mind at that moment. "You've been watching too much TV, Joshua," she would have lectured. "This is Grandville, Illinois, not the Himalayan Mountains."

Well, at the rate my life was going, I'd probably never see the Wisconsin Dells, much less the Himalayas. We couldn't afford a vacation this summer. Even summer camp hadn't been in the budget. No wonder I was bored.

I turned down a street I'd never noticed before, James Court. The sidewalk was uneven, and chunks of broken cement made it seem like an obstacle course. This detour was no piece of cake.

To get some speed, I stood up to pedal. As I pushed my right foot downward to gain momentum, I heard a whooshing sound that could only mean one thing—a flat tire. Now what?

I looked up at the house that faced the sidewalk. My big adventure of the afternoon had ended at 816 James Court. It must have been quite a place once, but now it looked like a jungle. The wrought iron fence that bordered the sidewalk was choked with vines, and the yard looked like African World at Brookfield Zoo. The front steps, or what I could see of them, looked positively lethal.

I'd lived in Grandville for almost a year. How come I hadn't heard about this place?

I thought I saw a movement at one of the windows, but when I looked again, there was nothing but a faded curtain. The street was deserted, and the sun had vanished behind clouds. I had the strange feeling that someone was watching me, but I couldn't see another living thing. Even the bugs seemed to have vanished.

Standing still on James Court wasn't going to fix my flat tire, but I didn't have any better ideas. I'd gotten my last flat tire in Woodview, where we lived before my parents got a divorce. Dad fixed that one in his workshop. Now he lived too far away to fix a flat—or to do anything else, for that matter.

With Sonny out of town and Mom at work, I didn't have many choices, and they all involved walking. Lugging my bike all the way to the ice cream shop and back would be hard work, but there wasn't much else to do. I could almost taste the rich and refreshing coolness of my favorite flavor, butter pecan.

I decided to take the short cut through the tunnel under the railroad tracks. But once I'd settled on a plan of action, I wasn't in a hurry to leave. I laid my bike down and stood staring at the run-down house. Did anyone actually live there?

So far I'd encountered both adventure (the flat tire) and mystery (the deserted mansion) on my way to Coach's Corner. I decided that I'd better not hang around any longer or romance would jump out from behind a bush. That mushy stuff wasn't for me.

I leaned over to pick up my bike, and a flutter of movement at that upper-story window caught my eye. I gave a cry of surprise. The windows were covered with grime, but I could see a shadowy outline of someone standing there. I gave a half wave of my hand, but the person dropped the curtain and vanished.

I was curious. Maybe I could pretend to be selling magazines and ring the doorbell. But what if the door opened and the mysterious figure grabbed me and pulled me inside? I shivered, picked up my bike, and headed for town.

Back in familiar territory again, I waved to the mailperson. (I have to call him that even though he's a man, because my friend Tracy at school insists on it.)

"Hi, Joshua," he called. "Sorry I didn't deliver any important mail to your house today."

Last spring I'd written to the governor, and everybody in town seemed to know about it.

"Hey!" I called to him. "Wait up." I pushed my disabled bike as fast as I could down the sidewalk.

"That tire looks as flat as a pancake!" He laughed uproariously at his humor. It was a good thing he was delivering mail for a living and not telling jokes.

"Do you know who lives in that big house on James Court?" I asked. "The one with the jungle in the front yard?"

The mailperson pushed back his safari hat and wiped his brow with a grimy red bandanna.

"Shore do," he said. "I been deliverin' mail on this route in Grandville for twenty-five years." He turned and started to

11

push his cart on down the sidewalk.

"Wait a minute," I said. "Who?"

"Who what?" he asked.

I was beginning to feel as though I were talking to a five year old.

"Who lives in the house?" I asked.

"Aw, shucks, Joshua," he replied. "I can't tell you that."

"Why not?"

"Confidentiality," he said softly.

"What's that?"

He lowered his voice still further. "Can't talk about the people on my route."

"I don't get it."

"Well, how would you like it if I blabbed all the secrets I know about you to the neighborhood?"

"Whaddya mean?" I asked.

"Well," he drawled, "we mail carriers know an awful lot about the people we deliver mail to. We know where your relatives live, how often they write, if you haven't paid your bills, and where you keep your money. It's all stored up here." He tapped the hard surface of his safari hat.

I wondered if he remembered that I'd only gotten three letters from my dad in the whole year we'd lived in Grandville.

"And that's where it's going to stay," he affirmed, smacking his hat once more for emphasis. "You'll have to find out who lives at 816 James Court from somebody else."

"What if I asked you a question, and you could blink once if the answer's yes and twice if it's no?" I suggested. "You wouldn't have to say a word."

"I wasn't born yesterday, Joshua," he said. "My lips are sealed."

"Well, how can I find out who lives there?"

"Why are you so curious?" he asked.

"I saw somebody at the window," I said.

He pulled on his chin thoughtfully. "Well, I could give you a clue to help you solve your little mystery," he suggested.

"Yeah," I said. "Give me the clue."

"Start at the Grandville Historical Museum."

"Where's that?" I asked.

"Over on Main Street, two doors down from Studebaker's Leather Emporium."

I must have walked by there a hundred times, and I'd never seen any museum.

But the mailperson assured me it was there. "If you hurry," he said, "you can make it before the museum closes."

The Grandville Historical Museum was made of brick and set back slightly from the other buildings in the block. No wonder I hadn't noticed it before.

I pushed through the door and into a narrow room that seemed to go back forever. This place was nothing like the Museum of Science and Industry in Chicago, where we'd gone on a field trip in fifth grade. That was all marble floors and huge rooms; this museum was cozy and crowded and smelled like old wooden furniture.

I stood for a minute to let my eyes adjust to being indoors, then I cleared my throat loudly, hoping to get someone's attention. I wandered over to a display of old tools.

"May I help you?"

I jumped a mile at the sound of the voice. My mysterious afternoon was getting to me.

"Sorry I startled you."

I turned to see a woman coming out of a small cubicle across the room. She was wearing a flowing black dress, and her earrings and necklace jangled as she crossed the room.

"Hi, I'm Susan Bradby," she said. "I'm the director of the museum." She stuck out her hand.

I remembered my manners and shook her hand briskly, just the way my mom always tells me to. "I'm Joshua McIntire," I replied.

"What brings you here on a nice summer's day?" she asked. "Most kids only come here on field trips during the school year."

"I want to find something," I answered.

"Well, that's an admirable goal," she replied. "We've got lots of stuff to find." She flung her arm in the direction of some boxes on the floor. Her bracelets jangled as she moved. "We're rearranging some exhibits right now," she went on. "That's why things look a little chaotic."

"I want to find out about a house," I told her.

"Architectural research?" she said. "We have extensive histories of many of the houses in town."

"No, I want to know who lives in a certain house," I explained.

14

"Oh," she said. "That might be a bit more difficult."

I must have looked as disappointed as I felt.

"But not impossible," she said. "Tell me about the house."

"It's at 816 James Court," I said. "It's a big mansion that's all overgrown with weeds."

"Well, that one's no trouble at all," she replied. "I can tell you right now, that's the old Murphy place. I think Miss Murphy still lives there."

"How old is she?" I wondered aloud.

"At least eighty or ninety," she said. "I'm not sure. But we can always find out."

"How?"

"We have baptismal records from the churches and all of the newspapers going back to the late 1800s. There's bound to be an answer there someplace."

"I just wondered who she was and why the house looks so run-down," I said.

"I can tell you a few things," Ms. Bradby said, "but if you really want to know more, you'll have to do some research on your own."

That sounded good to me. Last year I'd done a project on toxic waste. I'd read books and magazines at the university library in Chicago where my aunt is a professor.

"Wow, that would be great," I said. "Right now?"

Ms. Bradby looked at her watch. "I'm afraid not. We're closing in five minutes."

"Aw," I said. I wanted to get started right away.

"The museum will be closed for the next few days, but

15

after school starts, you may come in any time."

"Gee, thanks a lot," I said. Mom was going to be proud of all the manners I'd remembered today.

Coach's Corner was just down the street, and now I really was hot and thirsty. Maybe I could get a drink of water with my cone.

Suddenly I wasn't bored any more. I was hot on the trail of the Mystery of Murphy's Mansion.

I had the table set and water boiling for spaghetti when Mom walked through the door. She greeted me with a smile.

"Well, I am impressed," she said. "Let's have a fast supper and go shopping."

"Aw, Mom," I protested. To me going shopping ranked second only to a trip to the dentist.

"For school stuff," she went on. "Your first day is Wednesday, and this is Friday already."

Only four more days of freedom, I thought.

I put the sauce in the microwave while Mom changed her clothes.

"Wait until you hear about the old house I found today!" I yelled to her.

"What old house?" she asked with alarm, as she walked back into the kitchen.

She had every reason to be worried. Since we'd moved to Grandville last summer, I'd had my share of problems. I seemed to attract trouble the way our garbage can attracted flies.

I told her about the Murphy mansion and my visit to the museum.

She relaxed when I told her the director was going to help me. "Well," she advised, "just don't get into any trouble."

The last days of summer went fast. There wasn't time to think about the Murphy mansion. Wendell came home from camp, we went to church, I finally cleaned my room, and I finished reading a book.

On Tuesday afternoon I was curled up in the branches of an old willow tree in the back yard—the perfect spot for escaping the scorching heat—and daydreaming when I heard a voice.

"Hey, Josh."

I was thinking about Dad and wondering if I'd ever get another letter from him. I could always hope.

The voice repeated my name. "Joshua McIntire, I know you're up there!"

It was Wendell.

"Let's ride over to school and find out whose class we're in," he said.

"Whaddya mean?" I asked, sliding down from my perch.

"They post the class lists on the school door at three-thirty today," he explained.

"Great," I said. "Then you have a whole night to worry about it."

"Aw, come on," he urged. "Don't ya wanna know?"

My bicycle was still out of commission. Mom had promised to take it to Walt's Mobil after she got paid, but for now I was on foot.

"How about a little side trip on the way?" I suggested.

"What did you have in mind?"

"I found this really neat old house," I explained. "I'm going to do research on it at the historical museum."

Wendell looked suitably impressed. "Okay," he agreed. "Let's go."

We took turns kicking a smashed Coke can down the sidewalk. While we walked, I told him about the house.

"It looks just like you said," he enthused as we approached the Murphy mansion.

"Look real close at that window up there." I pointed. "That's where I saw somebody watching me."

"There's nothing there now," Wendell said, as he shaded his eyes from the sun to look up. "Maybe it was your imagination."

"No," I said emphatically. "Somebody was watching me."

We stood for a minute in front of the house, kicking at the chunks of cement that littered the broken sidewalk, but no one appeared at the window.

"C'mon," said Wendell. "Let's go."

A crowd of kids and parents was gathered around Jefferson's front door. We could hear exclamations of excitement and moans of disappointment.

19

I had mixed feelings myself. There were two sixth-grade teachers. Mr. Shonkwiler was sort of a comedian and told great stories, but he assigned tons of work. Mrs. Connell was new last year and had a reputation for being a strict disciplinarian. Some choice. Hard work or discipline. I wished the summer wasn't over.

Wendell and I waited our turn to stand in front of the door. He read faster than I did, and before my eyes had even focused on the tiny print, he gave a shout of glee.

"We're together! And we've got Shonkwiler!"

"Where's Ben?" I asked. If Ben Anderson was in Mrs. Connell's room, we'd all get more work done.

"In 6C," Wendell affirmed. "So's Samantha."

"Looks like the principal doesn't like Mrs. Connell very much," I speculated.

"There's a new girl in our room," Wendell observed. "Candy Stephens. I wonder where she's from."

"I wonder why anybody would name their kid Candy," I said.

I checked the lists to see where Trevor Monroe was. We'd been in Mrs. Bannister's class together in fifth grade, and I felt responsible for him. He has Down's syndrome, and sometimes kids make fun of him. Finding his name on Mr. Shonkwiler's list gave me a good feeling.

As I prayed before bedtime, my mind wandered. I have that problem sometimes. I'll be talking to God and all of a sudden I'm thinking about my dad. But this time I was worrying about school. Did I have the right supplies? Would I be able to do all of the hard sixth-grade work?

Please let this be a good school year, God. I don't want to get into any trouble.

And please won't You get my mom and dad back together? You're supposed to be able to do anything. Please come through for me on this one.

I prayed that prayer almost every night, but God didn't seem to hear.

The playground looked the same as last year. All of the teachers were carrying big posterboard signs, decorated with their names and cute pictures and fastened to sticks. The first grade teachers had purple dinosaurs on theirs. The whole scene looked just like a political convention.

But the difference was that this year I knew what was going on. Being new last year had been a bummer.

I didn't have any trouble finding Mr. Shonkwiler. Instead of carrying a cardboard sign, he was waving a flag. It looked like an old bed sheet and had a big black 6S in the middle. He was wearing bicycle shorts and a helmet.

"Hi, Josh-o," he greeted me. "Ready for sixth grade?" He raised his right hand to give me a high-five, and I reciprocated. He was certainly nothing like Mrs. Bannister.

I noticed the new arrival on the playground immediately. Was she a kid or a teacher? I wasn't sure. Either way, she stood out in the crowd. Even Mr. Shonkwiler's head turned.

"I think that's Candy Stephens, the new girl," I heard

21

someone whisper.

Most kids wore T-shirts and gym shoes to school. Even Wendell didn't dress as oddly as he used to when I first came to Jefferson. But Candy Stephens was definitely overdressed. Her earrings and high heels could have been borrowed from her mother, and at Jefferson nobody but the teachers wore lipstick. Was she serious?

"Wow," said Wendell. "How does she walk on those things?"

"Wait until she has to run the mile in gym," I answered. "Mrs. Borthistle will freak out."

"Man," said Wendell. "She can't be in the sixth grade."

"Stop staring," I said. "It's not polite."

I couldn't believe that I, Joshua McIntire, was actually reminding Wendell about his manners. Wait until Mom heard about this.

The bell rang, and Mr. Shonkwiler led our class into the building. Wendell needn't have worried about Candy. She walked confidently on her heels.

The classroom reminded me of Tropic World at Brookfield Zoo. There were green plants everywhere, some as big as trees. Tropical fish darted about in a giant aquarium near the window. There were so many shelves of books, it looked like a library. Mr. Shonkwiler's ten-speed bike was parked in the corner. And the overhead projector was mounted on top of a big barrel on wheels, instead of on the usual metal cart.

Mr. Shonkwiler took off his bicycle helmet and hung the

strap over the handlebars. Somebody said he rode fifteen miles round trip from home every day. Maybe he knew about repairing flat tires.

"Welcome back, everybody," he greeted us. "How was your summer?"

No one answered.

"In case you haven't heard, I'm Mr. Shonkwiler," he said. "But you can call me Mr. S."

I liked him already.

"Don't think it'll be all fun and games in here," he said. "I'm going to make you work harder than you've ever worked before."

A collective groan went up from the group.

"Well, you're alive," he said with a laugh. "I was beginning to wonder."

A hand went up across the room. It was Candy's.

"Like what kind of work?" she asked with a slight whine in her voice. She really had nerve. She looked like she was deciding whether to leave or stay.

"Well, you're going to do more writing in this class than you've ever done in your life," explained Mr. Shonkwiler. "You're also going to do lots of research."

Another groan went up.

"But we'll have a good time," he went on. "I believe that learning should be fun."

Candy didn't bother to raise her hand this time. Man, she was really monopolizing the conversation.

"What happens if you don't do the work?" she asked. The

whine was still there.

Mr. Shonkwiler looked a little exasperated. That was one of the good words I'd learned last year in Mrs. Bannister's class. My mother gets exasperated when I don't clean my room.

"Everyone works in here," Mr. S answered with authority.

Candy didn't look convinced. She slouched in her chair, tapped her fingernails on the desk, and glared at Mr. Shonkwiler, who just ignored her.

"Mr. Shonkwiler, may I have your attention, please?" The voice from the loudspeaker startled everyone. "Please line up your class and proceed to the gym."

"Oh, I forgot. We have an assembly," said Mr. S. "Let's get going."

Our class was the last one into the gym, and as we took our places on the chairs provided for sixth graders, I relished the feeling of finally being an important person at Jefferson. All the little kids had to sit cross-legged on the floor. This was the life.

Our principal, Mrs. Raymond, reviewed the rules and gave us a pep talk about getting good grades. Then she got very serious.

"I have some very sad news for you," she said. "Jefferson School is going to be closing at the end of this year."

I felt a giant lump in my throat.

"It's too crowded and small," she explained. "We need a bigger school."

I couldn't figure out why I felt so bad. After all, I wouldn't even be going to Jefferson next year—I'd be in junior high.

"We'll be in a new school next year," Mrs. Raymond went on. "Brand new and beautiful." But no one in the gym looked very happy.

Back in the classroom, Candy took over the conversation again.

"What's everybody so upset about?" she asked in that same whiny voice. "It's just some crummy building."

Before I knew it, my anger spilled out. "Shut up!" I shouted at her.

Mr. Shonkwiler raised his hand. "Wait a minute, here," he said.

Wendell reached over and put his hand on my shoulder. "Just ignore her," he advised.

But it was too late. The tears were already running down my cheeks. I left my desk and ran out into the hall.

So much for a terrific school year. I'd already embarrassed myself in front of the whole class. But how come I was crying and nobody else in the class seemed to care?

I didn't see the figure in front of me until it was too late. We collided with a bang.

"Joshua!" a voice said. "I hoped I'd run into you today, but this wasn't quite the encounter I had in mind."

It was Mrs. Ellison, the social worker. Just the person I needed. She'd helped me out last year.

"I guess you've heard the news about Jefferson closing," she said.

I nodded sadly.

25

"Would you like to talk about it?"

We sat down on one of the benches that stretched the length of the hall. I explained about Candy and what had happened.

"Do you think you can go back to class now?" she asked. "We could talk more during your lunch period."

"Okay," I agreed.

When I walked back into class, Mr. Shonkwiler looked upset too.

"This is going to be tough for all of us," he was saying. "But right now we have work to do. We'll talk about it more later on."

He wiped his eyes, and I suddenly felt much better. I wasn't the only boy who was crying.

"Let's go over some of the rules of the road," he said. "That's figuratively speaking, of course."

Boy, I'd have to pay attention if I was going to keep up with what was going on in Mr. Shonkwiler's room. He sounded as if he were speaking another language.

"Let's talk about your first writing assignment," he said. "Everyone's going to have a pen pal this year."

We all looked blank.

"Pen pals are friends that you write to regularly. Sometimes they live in a foreign country, but they could be students in a school on the other side of Grandville."

Man, was this great. I loved to write letters. In fifth grade I'd written letters to the governor of Illinois and to a cartoon character named McGee—and both of them had answered.

Maybe Governor Henry would be my pen pal.

"Your pen pal has to be someone you've never written to before," Mr. Shonkwiler continued.

Well, that eliminated the governor and McGee.

"I have a list of names you can choose from," he continued. "Or you can find your own. But you'll need to decide today. We're writing our first letters after lunch."

The morning flew by. New textbooks, more assignments, class rules, art class. But I only thought about one thing—who I would choose for a pen pal. I wanted somebody different. Somebody mysterious and special.

I thought about the book I'd read this summer, *Dear Mr. Henshaw*. The boy in that book wrote to an author. Maybe I could do that.

Nah, that wasn't mysterious enough.

Suddenly it hit me. I would write to Miss Murphy, the lady in the mansion.

Having lunch with Mrs. Ellison turned my day around. She reminded me of a conversation we'd had last year about God helping us get through the rough times in our lives.

"I don't understand why I get so mad and do dumb things," I said. "I thought I was over that."

She laughed. "Everybody has their problems, Joshua."

I couldn't imagine Mrs. Ellison doing anything dumb.

"The most important thing is to keep talking to God every day," she reminded me. "That way He'll help you do exactly what you're supposed to be doing."

I went back to class eager to write to my pen pal. I had lots of questions for Miss Murphy.

"I'll be giving everyone a stamped envelope," said Mr. Shonkwiler. "But after today, you'll have to buy stamps from our class post office."

The class settled down to write while Mr. Shonkwiler passed out the envelopes.

Dear Miss Murphy,

My name is Joshua McIntire and I'm in the sixth grade at Jefferson School. I'd like to be your pen pal.

That sounded dumb. I crumpled up the paper and took out another sheet.

Dear Miss Murphy,

We've never met, but I think you know me. I'm the boy who had a flat tire in front of your house. Why don't you get your sidewalk fixed?

Maybe this wasn't going to be as easy as I'd thought.

Dear Miss Murphy,

My name is Joshua McIntire. We've never met, but I think you've seen me. Remember the boy who got a flat tire in front of your house? That was me. I'm in the sixth grade at Jefferson School, and I'd like to be your pen pal. Some of the kids in the class are writing to people in foreign countries, but I think you will be more interesting.

I really like your house. How long have you lived there? Have you ever lived anywhere else? Do you work someplace?

Here are some important facts about me. I am eleven years old. I have lived in Grandville for one year. My parents are divorced. I take karate lessons and have a job at Studebaker's Leather Emporium. I get pretty good grades in school. I

only have one problem—sometimes I make the
wrong choices about things.

Please write back soon.

Sincerely,
Joshua McIntire

I folded the letter and slipped it into the envelope.

"Let's have all eyes up here on Rolling Thunder," Mr. Shonkwiler instructed. That's what he called his rolling barrel because it made a thunderous noise whenever he pushed it across the room. It was painted orange and blue. He was probably a Chicago Bears fan.

"I want you to use this form when you address your envelope," he told us. He put a sample on the overhead projector.

I knew the address by heart and wrote it carefully on the envelope.

Miss Murphy
816 James Court
Grandville, Illinois 60185

Then I put my address in the upper left-hand corner.

Joshua McIntire
631 Kinney Avenue
Grandville, Illinois 60185

"There'll be a prize for the person who receives the first reply," Mr. Shonkwiler said.

I hadn't sealed my envelope yet, and I pulled the letter out and wrote:

P. S. Please write back ASAP. I might get a

30

prize if you do. Thank you.

Mr. Shonkwiler collected the envelopes and promised to mail them after school. I noticed that Candy didn't turn one in, and I wondered what would happen to her.

"Before we close up shop for today," he said, "I'm going to explain a little bit about the research projects we'll be doing this year. You've probably done projects in other classes."

I nodded. I'd done three last year: cockroaches, the Underground Railroad, and toxic waste. Every one had gotten me into some kind of trouble.

Mom wouldn't be happy to hear about a new project. Maybe she'd write a note to Mr. Shonkwiler and get me excused.

Candy sounded as though she might be looking for an excuse too. "What if we don't know how to do research?" she asked. She still had that nasty whine in her voice.

"I'll be glad to ask someone to help you," Mr. Shonkwiler said.

Wendell looked across the aisle at me and rolled his eyes.

"What will make this project different is your hypothesis," the teacher continued.

My head was beginning to ache just thinking about this year. What in the world was a hypothesis? It sounded like some kind of strange disease.

Mr. Shonkwiler must have read my mind.

"A hypothesis is a statement you make at the beginning of your project about something that you think is true. During your research you're going to either prove or disprove your hypothesis."

I looked over at Candy. She was filing her fingernails.

"Let me give you an example," Mr. Shonkwiler said.

Thank goodness he wasn't going to leave us hanging.

"Suppose you were going to do a report on an endangered bird or animal. One hypothesis might be that the reason a certain animal is endangered is that man has destroyed all of the places where that animal can live."

My eyes began to glaze over.

"Another hypothesis to explain the disappearance of the animals might be that the food supply for that animal is no longer available, or it is contaminated."

Mr. Shonkwiler hadn't been kidding when he said we were going to work this year. I'd probably have to quit my after-school job at Studebaker's.

I thought about doing my project on the Murphy mansion, but where in the world would I get a hypothesis? While Mr. S. continued to talk, my mind wandered. Suddenly I got what a hypothesis was. It was like solving a mystery. The Mystery of Murphy's Mansion.

All I had to do was figure out some possible reasons for the house being so run-down and decide which one was most likely. Maybe Miss Murphy didn't have any money. Or maybe she wasn't into yard work. She might be too tired or sick to mow the grass. Maybe she did something else in her spare time. Or there was always the possibility that she hated the house.

"Any questions, class?" Mr. S. asked. "Don't worry if this all seems clear as mud." He laughed. "I'll go over it again tomorrow, and the next day, and the day after that."

The class breathed a sigh of relief. We were exhausted.

"Could I interest anybody in a cold can of pop?" Mr. Shonkwiler asked. He opened a portable refrigerator behind his desk and began tossing cans through the air.

The class came to life again. I caught a Coke and popped it open.

"There ought to be some reward for heavy-duty thinking. Right, Joshua?" Mr. S. smiled at me. How did he always know what I was thinking?

When the bell rang we were all laughing and talking.

I looked up to see Candy heading in my direction. Why me?

"Is this guy for real?" she asked. She had a slight sneer on her face.

"Whaddya mean?" I replied.

"What I mean is, do we really have to do all this work?" she asked. "I didn't do anything in fifth grade, and it didn't make any difference."

I wasn't sure how to reply to this revelation. I'd really worked hard in Mrs. Bannister's class.

"Where did you go to school?" I asked.

"We moved from out west," she answered. "My mom and her boyfriend just split up."

"Well, I think you'll have to do the work here at Jefferson," I said. "Mr. Shonkwiler has a reputation for being pretty tough."

"Well, I'm tough too," Candy said.

She turned and walked down the hall, her heels making a clicking noise as she went.

I could hardly wait to see what she'd wear tomorrow when we had our first gym class.

"Whaddya doin' now?" Wendell asked. He stuffed some papers into his backpack and followed me out into the hallway.

"Two things," I said. "Stopping by Sonny's place and going to the historical museum."

"Can I come?" he asked.

"Sure."

"Boy, that Candy is something else, isn't she?" he commented.

I'd never known Wendell to notice a girl before.

"She's different, that's for sure," I agreed. "I can hardly wait to see what happens when she doesn't do her work."

"I think we should invite her to Awana," said Wendell. Awana is a club we go to at Wendell's and my church.

"Aw, Wen, get serious," I said. "She wouldn't come to Awana."

"How do you know?" said Wendell.

"For one thing, she'd never be able to play games in that get-up," I said. "She'd probably break a leg."

"Let's see what she wears tomorrow," suggested Wendell. "Besides, you can't always judge people by their clothes." He gave me a sly smile.

I'd teased Wendell a lot about what he wore last year. When I first moved to Grandville, he didn't even own a T-shirt.

"You got me to wear different clothes," said Wendell.

34

"Why not Candy?"

"Aw, Wendell, she's a girl."

"I know," said Wendell with another smile.

The door to Studebaker's Leather Emporium was standing open, and we could hear the music from outside.

"Well, if it isn't that famous duo from Jefferson School," Sonny greeted us. "Long time no see." He leaned down and gave me a hug.

It felt good to see him again. I'd missed talking to him.

"Have I got some terrific news for you, Josh," Sonny said with a grin. "We're going to be famous."

"Who's going to be famous?" I asked.

"The King's Messengers," said Sonny. "We've been offered a recording contract and a big concert appearance in Detroit."

"Wow," said Wendell. "That's cool."

All I could think about was what it meant to me. "Are you going to move to Nashville?" I asked.

"Why in the world would I move to Nashville?" Sonny asked.

"A lot of famous singers live there," I said.

"I'm not going anywhere but Detroit for a weekend, and if your mom says it's okay, I'm going to take you along."

"No kidding," I said. "How come?"

"I'm going to hire you," Sonny said. "You're a good worker, and we can use some extra help at the concert."

"Do you really think my mom will let me?" I said.

"I am prepared to do a first-class job of arguing your case," Sonny said. "This concert is over the Columbus Day weekend, so the timing is perfect. You'll have Monday to recover from the trip."

"Could you use two helpers?" asked Wendell. "I've never been to Detroit."

"Yeah," I said. "Could Wendell come, Sonny?"

"I'll have to check with the other band members," said Sonny. "They agreed to Josh, but I'm not sure how they'd feel about two kids."

"Wendell's not really a kid," I said. "He's smarter than most grown-ups."

"You don't have to convince me," said Sonny. "Wendell's tops in my book. Let me see what I can do."

"First you have to convince my mom," I said.

"We've gotta go, Josh," Wendell interrupted. "If you want to stop by the museum, we've only got a few minutes."

"See you tomorrow," I told Sonny.

"I'm calling your mom tonight," said Sonny. "Don't spill the beans."

Wendell and I talked non-stop as we walked down Main Street to the museum.

"Do you really think we'll get to go?" Wendell asked.

"I'm not sure," I said. "But Sonny's a very persuasive guy."

We pushed through the museum's front door. Ms. Bradby was putting up a display and turned to greet us.

"Well, hello, Josh," she said. "I was wondering if you'd be in again."

"This is my friend Wendell Hathaway," I said. "Today was the first day of school, and we're on our way home."

"Hello, Wendell," she replied. Then she turned to me. "So, what have you decided about the Murphy mansion?"

"I'm for sure going to do something," I said. "But I'm trying to figure out how to work in this thing called a hypothesis that Mr. Shonkwiler says we have to have."

"If you can come in this Saturday," Ms. Bradby said, "I can set aside some time to talk with you. I have a couple of ideas that might help."

"What time?" I asked.

"Nine o'clock would be perfect."

Wendell and I ran almost the whole way home. I was anxious to see Mom. I had so much to tell her. Then I remembered that I couldn't tell her about Detroit yet. But there was Mr. Shonkwiler's class, the new girl Candy, and my mysterious pen pal. It had been quite a day.

"I'll see you tomorrow," I told Wendell.

"Call me if you find out anything about Detroit," he whispered.

"What are you whispering for?"

"We don't want your mother to know," he said.

"Wendell, we're standing on the front porch. And besides, she's not even home yet."

"Oh," he said with an embarrassed shrug. "Well, call me anyhow. See you later."

I talked so much during dinner that I was still finishing up my hamburger when Mom was clearing the table.

"Well, you couldn't have packed much more into this day," she said as she began to wash the dishes.

I smiled to myself. I had managed to pack one more thing in: a possible trip to Detroit. But I'd leave that news to Sonny.

I'd expected Sonny to call my mom, but she didn't say anything while we were eating breakfast. I wolfed down my Cheerios and bananas and popped two slices of raisin bread into the toaster. It was a long time until lunch, and now I couldn't raid the refrigerator at mid-morning the way I had all summer.

"Do you think I'll get an answer to my letter today?" I asked Mom.

"You just mailed it yesterday," she said.

"I really want to win that prize. What if she doesn't answer?"

"Then you'll have to choose another pen pal," Mom said. "Stop fussing and go brush your teeth." She tousled my hair and planted a kiss on my head.

I put my dishes in the sink and headed for the bathroom.

"What are you doing after school today?" Mom called from the kitchen.

"Working at Sonny's," I yelled back. The words came out all garbled because my mouth was full of toothpaste.

"Don't talk with your mouth full," she called back, but I could hear the laughter in her voice.

"I didn't know that toothpaste counted," I teased, coming out of the bathroom.

My mom was laughing a lot more this year. She didn't seem as sad as when we'd first moved to Grandville. And she really looked pretty today. She had on my favorite red dress, and her hair was pulled back with a matching ribbon.

"See you tonight, Josh," she said as she went out the back door. Her job at Associated Foods was getting to be more interesting all the time. Sometimes she helped out in taste tests and brought cookies and cereal home for us to sample.

The doorbell rang, and I knew it was Wendell. We walked to school together almost every day.

"So, what did your mom say?" he blurted out.

"About what?"

"About Detroit, of course. What else?"

"Sonny didn't call," I replied.

Wendell looked devastated. "How come?"

"I don't know," I answered. "Maybe he'll call her at work today."

"I can't wait," said Wendell. "If you can't go, then for sure there's no hope for me."

"I'll tell you as soon as I find out," I promised.

Wendell kicked a stone down the sidewalk. "I wonder what Candy will be wearing today," he said.

"You sure are interested in her," I kidded. "Since when do you care about girls?"

"I don't," he protested.

He looked embarrassed, and I was sorry I'd said anything.

"Who did you pick for a pen pal?" I asked, changing the subject.

"I picked a boy from Bogotá, Colombia. His name is Miguel."

"What language does he speak?"

"Spanish," said Wendell. "But he studies English in school, and Mr. S said he'll understand my letter."

"Well, it's going to take forever to get an answer from him," I said. "You won't have a chance to win the prize."

"So who cares about a stupid prize?" said a voice behind us. "The teacher's just trying to trick you into doing the work."

I turned sharply and almost ran into Candy. She was wearing bright pink shorts and white cowboy boots. At least she'd left her high heels home today.

"He's just using positive reinforcement," said Wendell.

I couldn't believe Wendell. He was actually talking to her. And I didn't have a clue as to what he was saying.

"Well, it won't work with me," Candy declared. "I'm too smart for that."

"Well, there are some people who will work for extrinsic rewards," said Wendell.

Now I was really in over my head. But Candy seemed to know what was going on. Maybe she was smarter than she looked.

41

"Not me," she said again. "In my last school, my teacher said I was the most unmotivated student she'd ever met."

"No lie," said Wendell. He looked absolutely spellbound.

"C'mon, Wendell," I urged him. "Let's go play basketball."

"You go ahead," he said.

Candy gave me a sly smile. I walked away from them feeling strangely left out.

All I could think about all day was Detroit, and Wendell didn't help at all. Every time we had a chance to talk, he brought the subject up.

"Do you think Sonny's called your mom yet?" he asked.

"Stop bugging me, Wendell," I complained. "We'll find out after school." But I was just as eager to hear as he was.

When the bell rang, we ran to Studebaker's.

"Are you guys training for the Boston Marathon?" asked Sonny as we burst through the door.

"So, what's the verdict?" I asked breathlessly.

"I've got good news and bad news," he said.

"What's the good news?"

"I called her," he answered.

I figured out the bad news right away, and my face fell. "She said I couldn't go."

"Not quite that bad," Sonny said. "She has to check with your dad first."

"How come?" I asked.

"There's a paper she signed when they divorced that says you can't go out of the state without his permission."

42

"So there's hope," said Wendell. "I've got to get home, Josh. I'll call you later."

"I have something else to tell you about my conversation with your mom," Sonny said after Wendell left.

"What?" I said.

"I asked her to have dinner with me tomorrow night, and she finally said yes."

I felt like somebody had punched me in the stomach. "Finally?" I questioned.

He nodded. "Every time I've been back in town this summer, I've called her," he said. "And up until today, she's always said no."

"When have you called?" I asked. The phone had never rung when I was home.

"I've always called her at her office," he explained. Then he looked straight at me. "I know how you feel, Josh," he said.

"No, you don't," I argued.

"I can still be your friend if I go out with your mom."

"I know," I said. "But if you go out with my mom, that means she won't get back together with my dad."

"Oh," he said. "That's the problem, is it?"

"I've been praying they'll get back together again ever since I became a Christian," I explained.

"Isn't it about time you gave God a break on that prayer?" Sonny asked.

"Everyone says that," I said. "But if God loves me, why wouldn't He want me to be happy?"

"Well, you aren't the only person that's involved," Sonny

answered. "How about your mom? Is she happy?"

I remembered her laughter that morning at breakfast. "Yeah," I answered grudgingly. "I guess she is." I wondered if Sonny had anything to do with that.

"Why don't you ask God to help you be happy and accept what's happened to you?" Sonny asked.

The idea had been suggested to me before. I guess I was a slow learner.

"Think about it, Josh," Sonny said. "And meanwhile, do you think you could get this floor swept?"

I looked at the piles of leather scraps on the floor and grabbed a broom.

I felt awkward about facing Mom at supper. Would she tell me about Sonny? What would I say to her? I took the long way home, past the Murphy mansion.

I envisioned Miss Murphy coming to the front door and handing me her reply. Then I would get the prize for sure. But the house looked deserted. I couldn't put off going home any longer.

I whispered a prayer while I walked. "Dear God, please help me to be happy and accept the fact that Sonny and my mom want to be friends."

The words seemed to stick in my throat. But I said them anyhow, twice more. Maybe Sonny was right.

Mom was there when I got home, and she greeted me excitedly at the door. "Look what came in the mail today." She was waving a pink envelope that smelled faintly of perfume.

"It's from Miss Murphy. The return address is James Court."

I couldn't believe it. Mr. S. had just mailed those letters yesterday. I looked at the spidery writing that spelled out my name and address.

But then I noticed what was missing. "It doesn't have a stamp," I pointed out to Mom.

"You're right," she said. "How did it get delivered?"

"Maybe the mailperson will know," I said. I'd ask him the next time I saw him.

I tore open the envelope and unfolded the pink sheet inside.

"What does it say?" Mom asked.

"Her handwriting is hard to read," I said. "It's kind of old-fashioned. Can you read it?"

"Dear Joshua," she read.

> Thank you for your letter of August 27th. I hope this letter will arrive quickly enough for you to claim the prize you seem so eager to have.
>
> I do apologize for the inconvenience you encountered in front of my house. That sidewalk is rather nasty, isn't it?
>
> The questions you asked in your letter are of a personal nature, and I do not wish to answer them. I would be happy, however, to correspond with you if you can contain your somewhat inquisitive nature. I enjoy discussing literature, the arts, and theater.
>
> I remain,
>
> > Yours truly,
> > Elizabeth M. Murphy

"What does it mean to 'contain my inquisitive nature'?" I asked.

"It's a polite way of telling you to mind your own business," Mom explained. "She has you all figured out after only one letter."

"Well, at least she'll be my pen pal," I said excitedly.

"I'm not quite sure how she's going to discuss literature, the arts, and theater with an eleven year old," Mom said, "but I can't imagine anyone else winning the prize. By the way," she continued, "just exactly what did you ask her in your letter?"

"I just asked how long she'd lived in her house," I said.

"I thought maybe you'd asked her how old she was," Mom said with a chuckle.

Even I knew better than that—although I've never understood what the big deal is about women and their age. I'm always glad when my birthday comes around.

The excitement of receiving Miss Murphy's letter had made me forget about Sonny's phone call. But the look on Mom's face told me she was about to bring up the subject.

"I've got good news and bad news," she said.

That was the same line Sonny had used. I wondered if they'd rehearsed their speeches together.

"What's the good news?" I asked.

"Sonny called me today, and I think the trip to Detroit is a great idea," she said. "I also think I can convince your father that it's okay."

I gave her a high five and a hug.

"Now for the bad news," she said. "Sonny asked me out on

a date, and I'm going."

We faced each other across the kitchen table, and she looked like she was about to cry.

"I'm sorry, Joshua," she went on. "This is something I really want to do."

"Relax, Mom," I said, surprising even myself. "It's okay."

The expression on her face changed to disbelief. "I've been dreading telling you all day," she said. "I was so worried about what you'd say."

"I felt the same way," I said. "I don't know what happened to change my mind."

"I think I do," she said. "Maybe we both had some help from heaven today."

"Could we eat dinner?" I asked. "I'm starved."

I couldn't wait to write another letter to Miss Murphy. I didn't care if she told me to mind my own business, I was still going to ask questions. I'd just try some different ones this time.

Dear Miss Murphy,

Thank you for writing to me so fast. I'm taking your letter to school tomorrow so I can get the prize. How did you get the post office to deliver your letter without a stamp?

Have you ever been to Detroit? I might go there in October with my friend Sonny. He's the drummer in a Christian rock band. He's going out on a date with my mother tomorrow night.

47

*Are you married or divorced? My mother is
divorced, and that's why she's going out with
Sonny. Do you have any children?*

I read what I'd written so far. There were quite a few
questions. Miss Murphy was right. I was pretty nosy. But
maybe when she got to know me, she wouldn't mind my
asking.

*My best friend is Wendell, but I'm worried
about him. All of a sudden he's interested in girls,
and you should see the one he's picked out. She's
something else.*

Please write again soon.

Your friend,
Joshua McIntire

"It's time to turn out your light, Joshua," Mom said. She
stood in the doorway of my bedroom holding a stack of
laundry.

"Thanks for being such a terrific son," she said and blew a
kiss across the room.

"Thanks for being such a great mom," I said. "I love you."

I hadn't said those words for quite a while, and once again
I was surprised at myself. Maybe God was answering my
prayers after all.

"I love you too, Joshua," she answered. "Now turn out
your light and get to sleep."

48

I was already awake, watching a spider crawl down the wall of my bedroom, when the alarm went off. The spider had been spinning a web up in the corner of the room and now was headed toward the floor. He didn't notice when the alarm went off, but I jumped a mile.

My mind was in a whirl. There was so much to think about today—the prize, my mom and Sonny, the trip to Detroit. My life had gone from boring to bombastic almost overnight.

The day was going to be another scorcher. Why did the weather always turn hot and humid just when school started? I didn't like having to take so many showers. I hoped Mr. Shonkwiler would have more pop in his refrigerator today.

"Josh, it's time to get up," my mom called into my room.

"Okay, okay," I replied.

Once my feet hit the floor, I began to get excited at the prospect of my prize. But then I thought about Sonny and my mom going out for dinner, and a knot formed way down in the pit of my stomach.

"C'mon, Josh," Mom called again. "Breakfast is ready."

I decided to wear my new Chicago Bulls T-shirt. I wanted to look good when Mr. Shonkwiler presented me with the prize. Maybe somebody would take a picture.

"Wendell's mom has invited you for dinner tonight," she said as she spooned scrambled eggs onto my plate.

"So where are you and Sonny going?" I asked with a calmness I did not feel.

"I don't know," she said. "I do know I'm nervous."

I looked at her in surprise. "How come?" I asked. "It's just Sonny."

"I haven't been out on a date for fifteen years," she said. "Not since your father and I started going out."

She looked a little sad, and I didn't know what to say.

"Well, Sonny is easy to talk to," I assured her. "Ask him about all of the famous people he's made stuff for."

I couldn't believe we were having this conversation. I was giving my mom advice about how to act on a date.

"Do you think he'll open doors for you?" I wondered.

"It doesn't matter one way or the other to me," she said. "What's important to me is that Sonny likes you."

I smiled broadly. This was a good time to remind Mom about Detroit. "Are you going to call Dad today?" I asked.

"I'll call on my coffee break this morning," she said.

"Are you going to tell him about your date?" I asked.

"That's none of your business, Joshua," she said sternly.

"I'm sorry, Mom," I said.

"Maybe Miss Murphy will help you curb your inquisitive nature," she said with a laugh. "Do you have your letter?"

I patted my backpack. "It's right in here, along with my reply. I'm going to buy a stamp from the classroom post office and mail it today."

"I've got to run, Josh," she said. "See you after school." Mom gave me a quick kiss and dashed out the door.

I sat alone at the kitchen table. I could see millions of tiny pieces of dust twirling around in a ray of sunshine. That's how I felt sometimes—like a little piece of dust twirling around and around.

Mr. Barron, our Awana leader, said that God cares about even the smallest flowers and birds. I wonder if He keeps track of spiders and flecks of dust. How does God manage to do all of that and still have time for the important stuff? Like making sure my prayers get answered.

A pounding on the back door interrupted my thoughts.

"Hey, Josh, it's time for school," Wendell called.

I opened the door. "Why'd you come to the back?" I asked.

"You didn't answer the front," Wendell answered. "I've been knocking forever."

"Aw, I was just thinking," I said.

"What about?"

"Just about stuff," I answered as we made our way down the tree-lined streets toward Jefferson.

He didn't ask any more questions, and I was glad. Instead, he switched to a new subject.

"So what do you think of the new girl?" he asked.

"Well," I said, giving myself more time to think, "she's interesting." That was the understatement of the century.

"I think she's fascinating," said Wendell.

I couldn't believe what I was hearing. Wendell thought Candy was "fascinating."

"Wendell, she's not your type," I stuttered.

"What do you mean?" he asked. Wendell was smart about some things. But he was really missing the point when it came to Candy.

"Well," I said, once again trying to figure out what to say. "You're really smart, and she isn't."

"You're wrong," Wendell argued. "She's very intelligent."

"Aw, c'mon," I said. "Look at the way she acts and dresses. You can't tell me she's smart."

Wendell didn't budge. "Just remember that you can't always tell a book by its cover."

I felt duty-bound to warn Wendell about the dangers of getting involved with the wrong friends. I'd had plenty of experience with doing that.

"I'm going to invite her to Awana," said Wendell. "Look what it did for you."

I wasn't sure how to take that remark. How could Wendell think I was like Candy? I'd never worn high heels to school.

Mrs. Bannister was on playground duty this morning. She called to me. "Good morning, Joshua. How are you liking sixth grade?"

I told her about my new pen pal and the prize I hoped to be receiving very shortly.

"I'm proud of you, Joshua," she said. "Keep up the good work."

I was embarrassed, but I remembered my manners. "Thanks, Mrs. Bannister," I said.

"You run along and get some exercise before the bell rings," she urged.

The minute I saw Mr. Shonkwiler appear at the sixth-grade door, I ran over.

"I got an answer to my letter!" I shouted excitedly.

He looked surprised. "Already?" he questioned. "Was it delivered by carrier pigeon?"

I remembered the unstamped envelope that Miss Murphy's letter had been delivered in and pulled it out of my backpack.

"Let's look at it when we get inside," he said. "We have to get the class lined up now."

After the pledge of allegiance, Mr. S. announced my triumph to the class.

"Josh got our first pen-pal reply," he said.

"That's impossible," said Candy.

She burned me up—she had a comment for everything. How could Wendell like her?

Mr. S. didn't seem to have heard her. He was holding up my letter for the class to see. "The interesting thing about this letter," he said, "is that it doesn't have a stamp on it."

"It's a phony," Candy said. "I'll bet he wrote it himself."

Mr. S. still continued to ignore her. Why didn't he just tell her to shut up? That's what I felt like doing. She was spoiling the whole thing.

53

"This letter gives us a perfect opportunity to hypothesize," Mr. S went on.

Oh, no, I thought. Here we go again. Why couldn't I just get my prize?

"Let's see if we can hypothesize some possible explanations for Josh's letter arriving so quickly and without a stamp."

He flipped the switch on the overhead projector and pushed Rolling Thunder to position it in front of the screen. Kids began shouting out possible answers.

Candy actually raised her hand, and Mr. S. called on her.

"He wrote the letter himself. It's a fake," she said.

I couldn't believe that Mr. S. wrote that suggestion down.

"The postage stamp fell off," someone else suggested.

"The letter was delivered by a uniformed messenger," Wendell said.

I looked at him in surprise. I hadn't thought of that. What a great idea.

Candy raised her hand again. She was participating just like a normal kid.

"Yes, Candy?" said Mr. Shonkwiler. "Do you have another suggestion?"

"Maybe the person who wrote the letter actually delivered it herself. Doesn't she live here in town?"

"Excellent possibility," enthused Mr. S.

I looked at Candy in disgust. What right did she have to talk about my letter?

"I can see you're getting the hang of hypotheses," Mr.

54

Shonkwiler said. "How are we going to find out which one is true?"

Cautiously I raised my hand.

"Josh?" Mr. S said.

"I could just ask Miss Murphy the next time I write to her," I said.

"That's too easy!" shouted Candy from across the room. She wasn't normal yet.

I glared in her direction. But at least she had dropped the idea that I'd faked Miss Murphy's letter.

"Asking her is worth a try," Mr. Shonkwiler said. "But see if you can do a little detective work first to test some of our other ideas."

"Okay," I agreed.

"But right now, it's time for the prize," he announced. "This is the first of what I hope will be many awards given during the school year. Whenever something special happens to someone, I give them one of these." He picked up a small box from the top of Rolling Thunder and handed it to me.

"Open it up, Josh," he urged.

I lifted the lid and took out a gold pen. Wow, this really was a prize.

"Read what it says."

"The owner of this pen is a Shonkwiler Student," I read.

"By the end of the school year, everyone will have won a pen," said Mr. Shonkwiler. "You are all Shonkwiler Students and will all do things worthy of this award."

I looked over at Candy. I seriously doubted that she could

ever do anything good enough to get a pen.

I pushed the point in and out several times and scribbled my name on a piece of scratch paper. I was going to write all of my letters to Miss Murphy with this pen. I would be a famous author with this pen.

I was helping Trevor shoot baskets at recess when I noticed Candy. She was looking strangely at Trevor, and I could tell she was wondering about him. Maybe she'd never met anyone with Down's syndrome.

"What's wrong with him?" she asked.

I frowned at her question and shook my head. Trevor may have a hard time understanding things sometimes, but he isn't stupid.

"I said, what's wrong with him?" she repeated.

She wasn't getting my message. Thank goodness the bell rang just then.

But Candy wasn't going to give up. She stood behind me in line and continued to press her question. "What is wrong with that kid?" she wanted to know. "He should be in a special class."

I thought Candy should be a in a special class, myself. But I owed it to Trevor to be polite and give Candy a good explanation. Maybe I could convince her that Trevor was just like we were.

Well, maybe he wasn't just like Candy. She had some real problems.

"Trevor has Down's syndrome," I explained. "Something

56

is different about the cells in his body, and it makes him look a little different and have a harder time learning things."

"He sure does look different," said Candy.

"Well, so do you," I snapped. I wasn't shouting and I wasn't angry, but my words had the same effect on Candy. She turned sharply and went to the back of the line. That was fine with me.

Friday night dinners at Wendell's were always the same—hamburgers, homemade French fries, and a butterscotch concoction for dessert. Mrs. Hathaway layered butterscotch pudding, ice cream, and Grape Nuts cereal into tall ice cream dishes. She served it with long spoons, and I loved the mixture of crunchy and sweet.

I liked Wendell's dad, too. He prayed before we ate and read from the Bible after dinner. He had a slow and deliberate way of reading that helped me understand. He wore brown pants with suspenders and floppy bedroom slippers.

Mr. and Mrs. Hathaway teased each other a lot, and Mrs. Hathaway always rested her hands on her husband's shoulders when she stood behind his chair.

"So what's this I hear about you winning a big prize?" Mr. Hathaway asked.

Wendell's little sister, Vanessa, giggled and tried not to open her mouth. She was seven years old and losing her baby teeth.

I pulled the pen out of my jeans pocket and proudly displayed it.

Vanessa smiled broadly, this time not even trying to hide the fact that she had no front teeth. "Tha's super, Josh," she lisped.

"So you're writing to Miss Murphy," Mr. Hathaway said.

"Yeah. Do you know her?"

"I went to high school with her nephew," he said. "She'd moved away by that time. Interesting family."

Wendell's eyes caught mine across the table. I knew he was thinking this would be a good time to bring up our trip to Detroit. I wondered if he had mentioned it to his parents yet.

"I might go to Detroit," I blurted out.

"Oh, really?" said Mrs. Hathaway. "Why?"

I explained about Sonny and the concert. The Hathaways didn't seem too impressed, but I went on.

"Could Wendell come with me?" I asked.

"Well," his mother said with hesitation. "We'd have to think about that."

Wendell smiled at me from across the table. She hadn't said no.

After dinner Mr. Hathaway did the crossword while the rest of us put a jigsaw puzzle together. Wendell's family didn't watch a lot of TV.

When the doorbell rang about nine-thirty, I knew who it was right away.

"That must be my mom," I said, jumping up.

"She's home pretty early," Mr. Hathaway said, as he went to open the front door.

I was right, but it wasn't just my mom. She had Sonny with

her. I hardly recognized him, all dressed up.

"C'mon in," invited Mr. Hathaway. "You can tell us about this Detroit trip the boys have been talking about."

I caught Wendell's eye and smiled. Maybe Mom's date with Sonny had served a purpose after all.

It was Saturday and I could have slept in, but once again I was awake before the alarm went off. I was too excited to sleep. Sonny had miraculously convinced Wendell's dad that a trip to Detroit was just what Wendell needed. He told Mr. Hathaway it would broaden Wendell's educational horizons, whatever that meant. And my dad had said the trip was okay with him, too.

Mom was putting in some overtime at her office today, so I dropped a Pop-Tart into the toaster and poured myself a glass of orange juice. Ms. Bradby was expecting me at the museum this morning, and I'd promised Sonny a couple of hours at the leather shop.

I wondered what Miss Murphy was doing today. Maybe I'd walk by her house on my way to town and look for signs of life. I thought about riding my bike, but I wasn't going to risk my new tire on that broken-down sidewalk.

The humidity had blown away in a rainstorm, and the air

was crisp and clean. It was starting to feel like fall instead of summer. I felt like skipping, but decided against it. I didn't want to look like a little kid. But inside, I felt good. Wen and I were going to Detroit, and I was going to find out all about Miss Murphy at the museum.

When I reached the Murphy mansion, I saw a truck parked in the driveway. The lettering painted on the side of the truck said "Pete's Tree Service" next to a picture of a monkey climbing a tree. There was no sign of Pete. Apparently Miss Murphy was finally going to get her trees trimmed.

I looked at my watch and realized I'd be late for my appointment with Ms. Bradby if I didn't hurry.

"So long, Miss Murphy," I whispered under my breath. "Hope we get to meet sometime."

I ran the rest of the way to the museum, and when I pushed open the front door, I was out of breath.

"Good morning, Josh," said Ms. Bradby. "What's your hurry?"

"I thought I was late," I explained.

She ushered me into her tiny office. There were books, boxes, and files stacked everywhere. It reminded me of my bedroom.

"I'm sorry for the mess," she said. "We just don't have enough room. Now, refresh my memory about what it is we're doing." She pushed her glasses up on her nose as she spoke.

I told her about the research project and also about the pen pals. She was impressed when I told her about receiving the letter from Miss Murphy.

"Well, we have several different things going on here," she said. "This could get complicated."

I nodded.

"We'll need to look at baptismal records, newspaper archives, and architectural files."

I nodded again. This was great. Sounded like Ms. Bradby was going to do my whole project for me.

"But you'll be doing most of the work," she said.

My bubble burst.

"Doing what?" I asked.

"Reading old newspapers. Looking at pictures. I hope you've got good eyesight and lots of time. This could take a while."

"Mr. S. seemed to think the most important thing was to get a hypothesis," I said. "What's my hypothesis?"

Ms. Bradby scratched her head. "I'd like to meet this man," she said. "He sounds like a terrific teacher."

"Maybe you could come to my class sometime," I suggested.

"Sure," she said. "But back to the hypothesis. I think we can concentrate on the age of Miss Murphy's house for our hypothesis."

"I don't get it."

"Well, we could hypothesize that, based on the appearance of Miss Murphy's house, it was built in the early 1900s."

"How do you know?" I asked.

"By the design of the house and the kinds of materials that were used," she explained.

"I still don't get it," I said. "If you already know, then why bother?"

"Ah, that's the fun of it," she said. "You never really know until you do the research."

"So what can I do today?" I asked.

"Let's start by finding out how old Miss Murphy is," said Ms. Bradby. "Then we'll know if she's always lived in the house."

She motioned me toward a table at the back of the museum.

"You can start right here," she said, "with our old newspapers." She pointed to a pile of papers stacked on the table.

"What do I do?"

"I'd guess she's about ninety. Why don't you start with the birth announcements for 1902? I've got the papers all ready for you."

"The whole year?" I said in dismay.

Ms. Bradby laughed. "It's not as bad as you think. The paper was published every other week. That's only twenty-six issues to read. If you don't find it in this pile, I'll get the next year out of the archives. Just make sure you keep them in order."

I picked up the first paper and breathed in that old-newspaper smell. *The Grandville Press*. It was dated January 4, 1902. I turned the fragile pages carefully, noticing the ads for Carter's Little Liver Pills and syrups that promised to cure consumption, cartarrh, and grippe. People sure had weird diseases back then.

I found the birth announcements on page twenty: Grace Volz, Margaret Bollweg, and Pearl Bartsch. No Elizabeth Murphy. I picked up the next paper and tried page twenty again. Sure enough, there were the birth announcements. This would make my search go faster.

I'd finished nineteen papers and was getting discouraged when I found her name. Elizabeth Murphy. Born September 26, 1902 to Cecilia and Edward Murphy. It was hard to connect this birth announcement with the person I'd imagined Miss Murphy to be. Her birthday was coming up in a couple weeks. Maybe I could get her a card.

"How's it coming?" Ms. Bradby called from her office.

"I found it!" I shouted.

"Terrific," she said, coming back to my table.

I beamed. "Now what?" I asked.

"Let's call it a day, and you can come back next week to look in the architectural files. Meanwhile I have homework for you."

She handed me a thin book. *Researching Your Illinois House: Compiling a History of Your 1820-1920 Home*.

Wait until I told Miss Murphy I was researching her house. Maybe she'd help.

"See you next week, Josh," Ms. Bradby said.

I stopped in at Coach's Corner Confectionery and picked up some Eye Poppers and Tongue Splashers to stave off starvation. Then I headed for the leather shop.

"Hi, Josh," Sonny greeted me. "I'm glad you're here. Help

64

me find a piece to match this." He held up a torn leather coat.

I went right to work. The two hours passed quickly, but my stomach was beginning to growl.

"How about a hamburger?" Sonny asked. He dug into his pocket and pulled out a ten-dollar bill. "Run down to King Cone and pick up some burgers and root beer floats," he said. "I'm starving."

While we ate, I tried to figure out a way to ask about his date with my mom.

"So, you're wondering if we had a good time?" he asked.

"Whaddya mean?" I said.

"I know what you're thinking," he said. "You're dying to know about my date."

"Well . . ." I said slowly.

"Don't deny it," Sonny said.

"Yeah," I admitted. "Mom didn't say much."

"She didn't?" Sonny asked. He looked worried.

"No, we just talked about Detroit."

"I took her to dinner at my favorite restaurant, the Mill Race Inn," he said. "We had a table by the window overlooking the river."

"Wow," I said. "That must have cost a lot."

"Well, I wanted to impress her," he said.

I couldn't believe this conversation wasn't bothering me.

"I've gotta go," I said. "I promised Mom I wouldn't be too late."

"See you next week," Sonny said.

I walked past Miss Murphy's on my way home. I wanted to

see if Pete had trimmed any trees yet. But the yard looked unchanged—wild and overgrown.

I stood in front of the house and concentrated on the upper-story window. Maybe if I waited long enough, Miss Murphy would appear again. Of course it could have been someone else I saw before. She might not live alone. After all, she'd been born in 1902, and that made her over ninety years old. No wonder her handwriting looked so frail. She was ancient.

I took one last look at the second-floor window. The curtain was pulled aside, and someone was watching me. I gave a little wave, but again there was no response. Then suddenly the curtain dropped and the figure was gone.

I checked the mailbox before I even put my key in the door. Underneath mom's mail there was a pale pink envelope. Like the first one, it had no postage stamp. But it was addressed to me in the now-familiar spidery handwriting and smelled faintly of the same perfume. I quickly tore it open.

> *Dear Joshua,*
>
> *I was hoping that you might be able to control your curiosity and not ask so many questions, but perhaps I was overly optimistic. Don't they teach you young people how to write declarative sentences in school anymore?*

I didn't know what optimistic and declarative meant. I'd have to get out my dictionary. But I got the idea that Miss Murphy wasn't going to answer my questions.

> *There, now you have a question of mine to answer.*

I am interested in hearing more about your studies in school. It is my considered opinion that schools today are lacking in discipline and academic standards. What is your opinion of this?

Oh dear, now I've asked you another question. Well, I have a proposition for you. If you can manage to answer the two questions I've posed for you, I'll answer two of the questions you've posed for me. I'll choose which ones, of course. The prerogatives of age, my dear.

I was going to need help in figuring out this letter. It was harder to understand than the Iowa Test of Basic Skills.

I've recently been rereading some old favorite books. Have you read Tom Sawyer *and* Huckleberry Finn? *There's another question for you; now I owe you three.*

I must be going, as I have some other correspondence to tend to. Please do write again soon. I'm enjoying this opportunity to "get in touch" with the younger generation.

Yours truly,
Elizabeth M. Murphy

I wondered what the M stood for. Her middle name wasn't included in the birth announcement. Maybe Mary or Margaret. There were plenty of those in the lists I'd read.

I gathered up the mail and went inside. I wanted to answer Miss Murphy's letter right away, but I wasn't sure I understood it all. I'd have to wait until Mom came home to help me.

As soon as I'd found out the trip to Detroit was definite, I'd pasted a calendar inside my journal and drawn a big red square around October 10. Now there was just one more day. I couldn't believe it was almost here.

I looked around the classroom. I was supposed to be writing in my journal. I noticed Candy wasn't doing anything either, as usual. Instead of writing, I flipped back through my earlier entries.

September 11: Got another letter from Miss Murphy yesterday. This one didn't have a stamp either. I still can't figure out how these letters are getting in my mailbox.

September 25: I bought a birthday card for Miss Murphy and mailed it. I had a hard time figuring out what to buy but decided on a Snoopy card that said, "You may be a year older, but you haven't lost your cool! Happy Birthday." Mom didn't think it was the greatest choice for someone who's over ninety, but I sent it anyhow. I wonder how it feels to be ninety-one?

September 30: Miss Murphy loved my birthday card. She said she hadn't received a card from a gentleman in years, especially from one who thought she was cool. Nobody's ever called me a gentleman before.

October 1: I did some more research at the historical museum. There was an article in a 1924 issue of The Grandville Times about Miss Murphy. It said that she graduated from art school and moved to New York City. She's never said anything about being an artist.

October 4: Yesterday Ms. Bradby gave me a neat "bird's-eye view" map of Grandville that was made in 1870. It was on a big sheet of paper and had all of the streets and houses drawn exactly the way they were then. I felt like I was in a helicopter hovering over the town. The big surprise was that I found Miss Murphy's house on the map. According to my hypothesis, it was built in the 1900s, so it shouldn't have been there.

Now I've got two mysteries to solve. Who's delivering Miss Murphy's letters to me? And why is her house that was supposed to be built in the 1900s on a map made in 1870?

I took out my gold Shonkwiler pen and began a new entry.

October 9: We're leaving first thing tomorrow morning. I can hardly wait. I've had my suitcase packed for a week. We're taking an old school bus that Sonny's band has changed into a traveling hotel.

When I woke up, it was dark and I could hear raindrops hammering on the roof. I didn't care. We were leaving, rain or shine. I slipped quietly out of bed and got dressed.

Then I looked at my clock that glowed in the dark. It said two o'clock! Just a little early. I lay back down on top of the rumpled covers. Only four hours to wait. . . .

"What are you doing all dressed?" Mom was shaking my shoulder.

At first I didn't understand the question.

She asked it again. "What are you doing all dressed?"

I sat straight up in bed and looked down at myself. Sure enough, I was all dressed. Then I remembered waking up in the middle of the night. When I explained my strange appearance, Mom laughed.

"Well, now it really is time to get dressed," she said. "Sonny's coming by for breakfast in a few minutes."

This was news to me. Sonny having breakfast at our house. Man, that would be different.

Mom outdid herself in the kitchen. French toast, scrambled eggs, bacon, and freshly squeezed orange juice.

"We won't have to stop for lunch until mid-afternoon with a breakfast like this under our belts," Sonny said, as he pushed away from the kitchen table. "Thanks, Charlotte. I really appreciate a good home-cooked meal."

She smiled at him in a way I hadn't seen her smile in quite a while.

"Run next door and tell Wendell it's time to leave," Mom said.

Wendell was at his front door waiting.

"Now you boys be careful," his mother admonished. "I know how you are with your adventures, Josh."

She reached over and tried to kiss Wendell, but he shrugged away.

"Aw, Mom." He looked embarrassed.

"C'mon, Wendell," I said. "We're ready to go."

"I can't stand it when my mother gets mushy," said Wendell as we crossed the lawn.

As I pushed through my back door, I saw Sonny and my mom standing in front of each other holding hands. I hesitated. They moved together and Sonny kissed her lightly.

I turned quickly from the door and ran smack into Wendell, who was right behind me.

71

"What's wrong?" he said.

"I can't stand it when my mother gets mushy either," I said sharply. "Especially with somebody else."

"Oh," said Wendell. He looked alarmed.

My breakfast felt like a lump of clay in my stomach. I'd barely gotten used to the idea of my mother going out with Sonny, and now he was kissing her.

They stepped apart when Wendell and I came into the kitchen. I pretended I hadn't noticed.

"Well, boys, are we ready to roll?" Sonny asked.

Wendell responded enthusiastically.

I could barely muster a one-syllable reply. "Yeah."

What a way to start the trip.

We loaded our suitcases into the bus that Sonny had parked at the curb. Where there should have been the name of a bus company, Sonny had painted "The King's Messengers." The seats had been removed from the back half of the bus, and he had built in bunk beds, a small bathroom, and a kitchen. The windows had curtains, and there was even a rag rug on the floor. It was just like the "Partridge Family" reruns on TV.

I should have been feeling terrific, but I couldn't get the picture of my mom and Sonny kissing out of my mind.

Wendell sat in the seat behind Sonny as we headed for Chicago to pick up the other band members. They chattered away as the bus bumped along on the expressway.

I sat at the back of the bus. I didn't feel like talking to anyone. I didn't say a word until we stopped for lunch.

"What's eating you, Josh?" Sonny asked as we headed

across the parking lot into the truck stop.

"Nothin'," I mumbled, keeping my head down.

"You can't fool me," Sonny persisted. "There's something bothering you, and I want to know what it is."

"I said nothing, " I repeated in a loud, angry tone.

"Well, I can't make you tell me," said Sonny. "But we're not going to have much fun on this trip if you're in a bad mood."

The tears welled up in my eyes. I didn't want to feel this way, but I just couldn't seem to control my emotions. Suddenly I was crying uncontrollably.

Sonny stooped down, faced me, and put his hands on my shoulders.

"You were kissing my mother," I said with a sob.

"Oh, so that's what it is," he said. "You're jealous."

"No, I'm not," I protested.

"Well, why else would you feel this way?"

I shrugged my shoulders. "I don't know."

"It's that old green-eyed jealousy monster that's got you in his grip," Sonny said. "You want your mother all to yourself."

I looked at him in disbelief. I didn't think I was jealous. But maybe he was right.

"You don't have to worry about your mom, Josh. She thinks you're the best thing since sliced bread."

"Really?" I said.

"You shouldn't even have to ask," he replied. "But I happen to know that she thinks you're the best looking, smartest, most well-mannered eleven year old in the whole wide world."

73

"She said all that?" I asked.

"Shore did," Sonny affirmed. "She told me that nothing in the world would ever come between her and you."

I managed a smile.

"Now, I hope you'll get your chin up off the ground and have some lunch," Sonny said. "We've got a ways to go before we get to Detroit, and you're going to need some nourishment."

After my talk with Sonny and a cheeseburger for lunch, I felt a lot better. The band members took turns driving while the others sat in the back and fooled around with their instruments and sang. I'd never had a chance to see Sonny's band up close.

The saxophone player was named Turtle. At least that's what they called him. I couldn't imagine anybody naming their kid Turtle. When I asked Sonny where the name came from, he said that Turtle's real name was Harold—as if that explained everything.

"I don't get it," I said.

Sonny smiled and whispered, "Just look at him."

I stared at Turtle, who was slouched low in his seat blowing random notes on the horn. He did look like a turtle. He was wearing a black turtleneck that rested in heavy folds around his very short neck. As he played, his chin seemed to disappear from time to time into the folds. And his eyes bulged out when he hit the high notes. It was a perfect nickname.

The guitarist, Ronnie, was also the lead singer. He was the youngest member of the group, and his T-shirt had a Bible verse printed on the back and a cross printed on the front. I'd never have the nerve to wear a shirt like that. He didn't say much, but could he sing. I remembered getting chills when I heard him for the first time.

But my favorite band member, other than Sonny, of course, was Steve, the keyboard player. There was something about him that reminded me of my dad, although I couldn't quite figure out what it was. He never seemed to be serious about anything, and his laugh started way deep down in his very generous stomach and then just rolled out of his mouth. He was always eating candy bars and, according to the rest of the band members, needed to go on a healthy diet. They teased him constantly about his eating habits.

I could hardly wait to be a grown-up so I could eat candy bars whenever I felt like it. I did have second thoughts, however, when I looked at the rolls of fat that spilled out over Steve's belt.

When we got tired of listening to the music, Wendell and I played the license plate game. We got up to twenty-seven in a couple of hours. Our best one was Mississippi. After we spotted it on a run-down red pickup truck, the guys in the band sang a song that Mom and I used to sing a long time ago. M-I-S, S-I-S, S-I-P-P-I. We ate the red licorice we'd bought at the truck stop, and Sonny brought out cans of pop from the refrigerator. It was like being on a desert island, only our island was bouncing down the highway at fifty-five miles an hour.

"You guys ought to take a little nap," Sonny suggested.

"A nap?" I questioned. "Naps are for little kids."

"Tough," said Sonny. "We're going to be up pretty late tonight, and we have a lot of hard work ahead of us. Just lie down and relax for a while, even if you can't fall asleep. And make sure you fasten your seat belts."

"In a bed?" I asked.

"Yes, in a bed. We had them especially installed for you guys. Your mother insisted."

Wendell and I went to the back of the bus. I climbed into the top bunk and fastened my belt. It was really a bed belt, not a seat belt. The last thing I remembered was Wendell pushing his foot into my back from below and asking, "Are you asleep yet?"

When I woke up, the bus was still bouncing along, but we were obviously much closer to our destination. There were tall buildings and factories outside the windows. It looked a lot like Chicago. I wondered how much farther we had to go.

"Hey, Wendell, are you awake?"

I got no answer and rolled to the edge to look over. The bottom bunk was empty. I jumped down and made my way to the front of the bus. I had to hang on to keep from falling. Those bed belts were a good idea.

"I thought naps were for little kids," Sonny said with a laugh. "I could hear you guys snoring all the way up here."

I told them how I'd gotten up at two that morning, and everybody laughed. I wasn't even embarrassed.

"Reminds me of the time you forgot to set your clock ahead when the time changed and showed up an hour late for a concert," Steve teased Sonny. "We had to stomp our feet on the

76

stage to keep time without a drummer."

"Well, that wasn't as bad as the time you got mixed up and started singing a totally different song from the rest of us," Sonny reminded him.

Everybody howled and slapped their knees.

I watched in amazement at these adult hi-jinks. I didn't know grown-ups ever had so much fun.

Turtle was driving the bus, and as he pulled into the parking lot of the Cresswood Concert Hall I could feel everybody's excitement beginning to build. This was a big concert for the band. Lots of important people would be listening.

Turtle eased the bus into a loading dock area, and Wendell and I waited eagerly for him to open the door.

"Hey, not so fast, you guys," he said.

"Whaddya mean?" Wendell asked.

"We always pray before we get off the bus," Turtle said. "There are a lot of things that can go wrong at a concert. Especially if we forget about the real reason we're here."

The band members all knelt down at the front of the bus. I looked at Sonny, and he motioned for Wendell and me to get down too.

Sonny prayed first. "Father, thanks for a safe trip and for the chance to sing here in Detroit. We thank You too for letting Josh and Wendell come along. Use this group to be Your true messengers tonight."

Each of the band members followed with a short prayer and when the last person said amen, I expected everybody to open their eyes and stand up. But there was silence. Then I heard Wendell praying. Surely they didn't expect me to pray too?

My heart began to pound. I'd never prayed in front of so many people. What if I said the wrong thing? The pounding got louder. I suddenly realized that Wendell was finished. Nobody moved. Well, here goes, I thought.

"Thanks, God, for letting us come on this trip." So far, so good, I thought. "Please help the band do a good job tonight." I was still in control. "Maybe there will be somebody at the concert tonight who needs to get to know You. I hope You'll be there to meet that person."

Suddenly I didn't know where the words were coming from. They didn't seem to be mine anymore. I'd forgotten how nervous I was. "Please help everybody in the band to play all the right stuff." Then I felt self-conscious again and abruptly ended my prayer. "Amen."

Everybody got to their feet almost in unison, and Sonny put his arm around my shoulder.

"Thanks for your prayer, Josh," he said with a smile.

I smiled back. I'd never felt so good in my life.

We made our way through a maze of hallways to the main stage. The concert hall was enormous. Wendell and I looked out over the darkened auditorium, and I imagined what it would look like filled with people.

"I think I've got stage fright," said Wendell.

"What?" I asked.

"It's when you're real nervous before you have to get up in front of people to do something," he explained.

"I know what it is, Wendell," I said, "but we're going to be sitting down there." I pointed to the front row.

"But now that I know the band, I think I'll have sympathetic stage fright," Wendell said.

"Where do you come up with this stuff?" I asked, rolling my eyes.

"I'm just brilliant, that's all," he answered with a grin.

"Did we bring you guys just to stand around and talk?" Sonny teased. "C'mon, we've got work to do."

He wasn't kidding. We began unloading the bus. The temperature was in the fifties, but perspiration began to drip down my face. Speakers, lights, instruments, suitcases, guitars, drums, cymbals. The bus didn't seem big enough to have carried everything we were now moving into the auditorium.

"Ronnie, how come you've got so many guitars?" Wendell asked. "You can only play one."

"I can only play one at a time," Ronnie explained. "But some songs just sound better with a different kind of guitar. It makes my music more interesting if I change off."

"Well, I've only got one saxophone," said Turtle. "I've had it since sixth grade. I don't know what I'd do if anything happened to it. It's just like my right arm."

"Actually it's much better looking than your right arm," teased Steve.

Turtle laughed and punched him playfully in his pot belly.

It was nearly five o'clock when we finished setting up the stage. The lights were in place. Controlled by a computer, they changed colors and positions automatically when Steve punched the right buttons.

"We've just got time to grab a quick dinner before we have to hide out backstage," Sonny said.

We ducked into a little diner across the alley from the auditorium. Once we got seated, there wasn't room for anybody else in the place. I wasn't sure I could even eat anything, but when Wendell ordered the meat loaf plate, I decided to go for it.

Steve prayed before we dug in to our generous platters of food. I couldn't help sneaking a peek while the others had their heads bowed. The waitress was watching us with a quizzical look. I hoped she was coming to the concert tonight.

The meat loaf was super. Almost like Mom's. I devoured every morsel, and Wendell matched me bite for bite.

"Are you sure you guys didn't inhale your food?" Steve asked when we were done.

It was dark outside when we crossed the alley again.

"Let's do a last-minute sound check," Sonny said, "and then I'll get Wendell and Josh settled in their front-row seats."

Even though it was early, there were already small groups of people gathering in the aisles when Wendell and I came from backstage.

"Remember the concert we went to when we first met Sonny?" I reminded Wendell.

He nodded. "I wonder if the people here will stand up and clap to the music the way they did that night. I remember some kids who raised their hands like they were reaching up to heaven."

The auditorium was filling up fast now. There was a buzz of excitement. I felt proud that Wendell and I were friends of the band.

The lights went down, and the concert began.

After the opening number, I looked over at Wendell.

"Wow," he said. "The seats were actually vibrating from the bass."

At the beginning of the next number, Steve encouraged everyone to clap along. It was then that I discovered something I'd never known about Wendell. He had absolutely no sense of rhythm. One thousand nine hundred and ninety-nine people were clapping together, and one person was clapping to the beat of a different drum—Wendell.

I tapped him on the shoulder and pointed to my hands. He tried desperately to match my clapping, but he couldn't do it. I shrugged and looked away. He was even getting me confused. I'd gotten Wendell to wear gym shoes and T-shirts, but I wasn't sure that anyone could help him in the rhythm department.

The crowd loved the band—especially the new number that Sonny had written. It was called "Another Chance," and it talked about how God is always willing to give us a second chance when we don't follow His commandments the first time.

After their last song, Steve introduced a special guest. At that first concert we'd attended, we heard a Bears football player tell how God had changed his life. This time the speaker was George Becker, a Detroit Tigers baseball player. He talked about how important it is to let God direct our lives and not think that we have to have all of the answers. He talked about how he'd gotten hit with a baseball and lost his eyesight for almost a whole year.

I couldn't imagine not being able to see anything for that long. Talk about trouble.

"We all spend far too much time worrying about things that we shouldn't worry about," he said. "If God cares about the birds of the air and the flowers of the field, don't you think He cares about you?"

I wondered how George Becker knew that I worried a lot.

"Make sure you lay those problems on God every day," he suggested. "He'll take care of them faster than a first baseman can throw a runner out at second."

I seemed to be getting this lecture quite a bit lately. "Don't worry. Let God handle it." It was good advice.

Sonny put Wendell and me to work again after the concert. We carried equipment, took down risers, and packed up lights. When we finally finished, it was nearly two o'clock in the morning.

We climbed back into the bus. "Pick a number for the bathroom," Sonny said. "Then we're hitting the sack."

I must have fallen asleep instantly. The next sound I heard

was Turtle's saxophone.

"Do you have to play that thing so early in the morning?" Steve called. "Give a guy a break."

"Would you rather wake up to my sweet music or an alarm clock?" Turtle teased.

"Okay, you guys, let's get moving," Sonny said. "After we have breakfast, we're on the road."

In the diner across the alley, the same waitress took our breakfast order. She looked exactly the same as yesterday, right down to the catsup stains on the front of her uniform.

"We'll have six of the special breakfast platters," Sonny said.

I quickly read the menu. Flapjacks, eggs, sausage, hash browns, toast, and orange juice. I was glad Sonny was paying the bill.

Once we pulled out onto the highway, the miles flew by. Wendell and I played the same games again, but mostly I sat and stared out the window. I was still tired from last night.

Mom was waiting when we got home. She greeted me with a big hug and a kiss, and I wasn't even embarassed. I noticed she didn't kiss Sonny, though.

"These guys were a terrific help," Sonny said.

"Did I get any mail?" I asked.

"Nothing," Mom said.

I was disappointed. I could hardly wait to tell Miss Murphy all about the trip.

"I'm going to walk over with Wendell," Sonny said. "You get some rest, Josh. See you later in the week." He squeezed my shoulder and gave my arm a little punch.

When they'd gone out the door, Mom said, "I want to hear all about your trip."

"What do you want to know?" I asked.

"Let's not play games, Josh," Mom said. "Start at the beginning and tell me everything."

Once I got started, I couldn't stop. I told her about sleeping in the bus and eating in the diner. Mom laughed as I told her about how much fun the band had together.

"They're an unusual group," she said. I wasn't sure if that was a compliment or not.

It was kind of quiet being home again. I missed all of the joking and teasing. Maybe I'd get to go on another road trip sometime soon.

At least the next day was Columbus Day, so I'd have plenty of time to go to the museum and stop by Miss Murphy's house. It worried me that I hadn't heard from her.

When I woke, the sun was streaming in my bedroom window. A quick look at my clock confirmed my suspicions. It was after noon. I'd never slept this late in my whole life. Should I eat breakfast or lunch?

I threw on some jeans and a T-shirt, grabbed a peanut butter and jelly sandwich, and headed for town. My first stop was 816 James Court. I don't know what I expected to find, but everything looked the same. I looked up at the second-story window once more. There was no one there. I decided to check out the back yard.

It turned out to be even more overgrown than the front. Untrimmed apple trees loaded with ripened fruit hung almost to the ground. Overturned rusty lawn furniture looked like buried treasure under a cover of weeds and grass. I imagined what it might have looked like long ago.

The bright sunshine did not penetrate the backyard jungle, and I shivered. Time to get out of here. This place was creepy.

I took one last look up the window. Still no sign of anyone. Where was Miss Murphy?

Even though the museum wasn't officially open, Ms. Bradby was there working. She came to the door when I knocked and invited me in.

"So, how was your trip to Detroit?" she asked. "I got my master's degree in social and behavioral sciences near there."

I had no idea what social and behavioral sciences were, but I wasn't about to admit my stupidity to Ms. Bradby.

"The trip was great," I said. "Now I want to find out some more stuff about Miss Murphy's house. That bird's-eye map showed that my hypothesis isn't working right."

"Well, there's always the possibility that someone did some renovations on the house," she suggested.

"What are renovations?" I asked.

"Miss Murphy's family may have remodeled and updated the house to make it look newer. People often do that to houses."

"What do you think they did to this one?" I asked.

"The front porch and brick pillars were probably added to

make it look like an original Foursquare House. They fooled us into thinking it was built in the 1920s."

"How can we find out for sure?" I asked.

"The best source of information would be our picture file," she suggested.

"More detective work?"

"Don't get discouraged," she said. "We're almost there. I can feel it."

I looked through two huge stacks of pictures. I was beginning to get an idea of what Grandville was like when Miss Murphy was a little girl.

I found what I needed in the third stack of photographs. There were two snapshots of the house, both labeled "816 James Court." The first showed the house as it looked in 1890. The hundred-year-old trees that surround it now looked like twigs in the picture. The second shot was taken in 1937. There was a family group in funny-looking clothes standing in the front yard. Was that Miss Murphy in the back row next to a man with a mustache?

Ms. Bradby's hunch had been exactly right. I hollered for her, and she left the display she was working on to come take a look.

"I think you've got it, Joshua!" she exclaimed. "If you could actually see the inside of her house, you might be able to see the structural changes that have been made. But these photographs are pretty good proof."

"I think they'll have to do," I responded. "Miss Murphy's pretty private."

I was curious to see the house again to compare it to the pictures I'd seen. I pedaled my bike back to James Court as fast as I could and stood in front of the house for the second time that day. Miss Murphy was probably going to start charging me rent for her sidewalk.

As I stared at her house, I could just imagine how the porch had been added. I wondered how it felt to live in one house your whole life. I thought about our old house in Woodview. Maybe the people who lived there now were putting on a big addition, and I wouldn't even recognize it. I still missed being there with my mom and dad together.

I looked for parts of the house that had been in the 1890 picture, but it looked completely different. I wished whoever had renovated it had left the neat little tower the picture had shown.

I decided not to wait until I heard from Miss Murphy. I was going to write her another letter when I got home.

I still had an hour before Mom got home from work. Just enough time to write my letter. Then I had an even better idea. I'd call Miss Murphy. That way I could ask her in person about seeing her house.

I hadn't had anything to eat since my combination breakfast and lunch, so I grabbed a slice of cheese and rolled it around a piece of ham. A breadless sandwich, I called it. That would hold me until dinner.

I pulled the phone book down from the shelf and turned to the M's. Mitchell, Morrow, Munster, Murphy. There weren't many Murphys in Grandville, only five, and there wasn't an Elizabeth among them. Then I checked the addresses that went with the names. There was an Edward Murphy listed at 816 James Court. That was her father's name. But he was dead.

I dialed the number and let it ring. Maybe she'd have an answering machine, and I could leave a message. I lost count after twenty-five rings and hung up. Maybe Miss Murphy was on vacation. That would explain the lack of letters. Of course, that must be it.

But I'd write her anyhow. There were a bunch of things I needed to tell her about my trip to Detroit and her house.

I finished off the meat and cheese in one big bite, wiped my hand on my jeans, and settled down to write.

Dear Miss Murphy,

I'm back from my trip to Detroit. It was great. Especially when Wendell and I got to sleep in bunks on the bus. Now I've visited ten states in my lifetime.

Are you on vacation? Where did you go? I tried calling you today, but you didn't answer. That's how I figured out you were on vacation. Hope you won't be gone too long.

Yours truly,

Joshua McIntire

I folded the letter and put it in an envelope. While I was writing the address, I remembered the mailperson. I bet he would know about Miss Murphy's vacation. Didn't people leave their mail at the post office when they were on vacation instead of having it delivered? Tomorrow night after school I'd look for him and check out my theory.

I was so engrossed in my mental detective work, I didn't hear Mom come in.

"Joshua, are you here?" Her voice echoed through the house.

"In here, Mom!" I hollered. "In my bedroom."

90

She greeted me with a big smile and a hug. "I missed you," she said. "It was quiet around here while you were gone."

It still felt pretty quiet to me, after being with the band on the bus. Over our bowls of steaming vegetable soup, Mom asked a lot of questions about Sonny and the concert.

While we cleared away the dishes, she continued to talk about him.

"How would you feel if I went out on another date with Sonny?" she asked.

"Why?" I wondered.

"Because I want to," she said. "He wants to take me to his concert at the college auditorium."

"So are you asking me if you can go?" I said.

"Absolutely not," she answered sharply. "I'm asking how you would feel if I went."

"So you've already said yes," I guessed.

"Well, yes, I did," she admitted.

"It's okay, Mom," I said. "Sonny and I talked about it on the trip, and it's okay."

We had to give an update on our reports to Mr. S during language arts class on Tuesday. I told him about the old newspapers and the picture file.

"Quite impressive, Joshua," he said. "Now you need to think about how you're going to write it all up in report form."

As I walked back to my desk, I heard Candy mutter under her breath, "Show off."

I couldn't wait for the day to end. All I wanted to do was

91

find the mailperson and check out what he knew about Miss Murphy.

Mr. S. was talking about trapezoids and rhombuses, and I was having a hard time staying awake. Even though he had all kinds of diagrams on the overhead projector, I still was confused. Math wasn't my best subject.

Wendell leaned across the aisle and poked me. "Candy's coming to Awana tonight," he said.

"Oh," I said. "That's nice." What was it with everybody? First my mom and Sonny. Now Wendell and Candy. And it wasn't even springtime. I felt like I didn't have anybody left anymore.

That reminded me that I hadn't heard from Dad since the middle of the summer. Well, I still had Miss Murphy. Or at least I thought I did.

"I'll pick you up at seven," Wendell said as we walked out of school.

"How come?" I said.

"For Awana," he said. "Earth to Joshua. Earth to Joshua."

"Okay, Wendell, don't bug me. I'll be ready."

"Do you have your memory work done? Our team needs the points."

"All right, Wendell, don't bug me. I'll be ready."

The calm I'd felt earlier when Candy was teasing me had just disappeared. Why was I so annoyed with Wendell?

I tried several streets before I found the mailperson. Or at least I found his three-wheeled cart parked in front of a house.

He was nowhere in sight.

Suddenly he appeared from behind a house. In spite of the cool weather, he was still wearing Bermuda shorts and that silly safari hat.

"Well, Mr. McIntire, how are you today?" he addressed me.

"I'm fine, thank you," I responded, remembering my manners. "May I ask you something?"

"Sure," he replied.

"About Miss Murphy?"

"Ah, I see you've done your homework," he said with a smile.

"I've been writing to her," I said. "She's my pen pal."

He got a funny look on his face. "I know."

"Yeah," I said. "You've been delivering her letters to my house. How come they don't have stamps on them?"

Now he looked even funnier—as though he'd been caught with his hand in the cookie jar.

"Well, that's an interesting question, Joshua," he said.

I felt like he was evading me. "I thought if letters didn't have stamps, you wouldn't deliver them," I said.

"We-ell," he said, drawing the word out. It was like he was the kid and I was the grown-up.

"How did those letters get in my mailbox if they didn't come from the post office?" I asked him.

"Well, I guess I'll have to spill the beans," he said. "One day when I was delivering Miss Murphy's mail, she asked me to do her a favor and drop your letter off. Said she didn't have any stamps in the house."

"Really?" I said.

"After that she'd stick her letters to you in her mailbox, and I'd drop them by when I delivered your mail. Those letters never even went to the post office."

"Wow," I said.

"I could lose my job over this," he continued.

"Nah," I assured him. "But how come I haven't been getting any lately?"

"I don't have a clue," he said. He looked a little agitated. "She hasn't emptied her box for quite a while."

"Maybe she went on vacation," I suggested.

"That's possible," he said. "But she didn't say anything to me or fill out a hold card at the post office."

"Has she ever gone away before?" I asked.

"Not since she moved back to Grandville four years ago," he said. "I've had her route the whole time."

"I'm worried," I said.

"So am I," he admitted, "but there isn't anything we can do."

I wasn't so sure about that, but I nodded in agreement. "See ya around," I said.

I just had time to run home and change into my Awana uniform before Mom arrived.

"Set the table and get out the cheese and bread," she requested. "We're having grilled cheese."

She called to me from the bedroom where she was changing her clothes. "I got another raise today, Josh. At this rate, we'll be able to take a little trip during Christmas vacation."

The doorbell rang promptly at seven. Wendell looked like he'd taken a shower and combed his hair. I thought I smelled hair gel, but I couldn't be sure.

"So, what are you all slicked up for?" I teased.

But Wendell wasn't playing my game. "My mother made me take a shower because I got sweaty playing outside before dinner," he explained.

When we arrived, Mr. Barron was already shooting baskets with some of the guys. My friend Tracy from school was talking with some of her girlfriends on the bleachers.

Wendell kept looking toward the door. I knew he was watching for Candy.

"Do you really think she'll come?" I asked him.

"She promised," he answered.

"I don't think she's real reliable," I said.

"I don't understand why you won't give her a chance," Wendell said. He sounded exasperated, which was unlike him.

"I just think she's trouble," I explained.

"Well, wait and see," Wendell said.

We didn't have long to wait. When Candy came through the door, every head turned in her direction. The outfit she'd worn for the first day of school was nothing in comparison to what she had on tonight. Her leopard-print stretch pants and black shirt made her look like something out of the jungle.

Wendell seemed oblivious to her outrageous outfit.

"See, what did I tell you?" he said. "She's here."

Even Mr. Barron looked a little uncomfortable with Candy's presence. He was used to T-shirts and blue jeans.

But Wendell just introduced Candy to everyone. I had to give him credit. Either he didn't care what anybody thought or he was going to win an Academy Award for best actor.

We recited our memory verses. I was a little embarrassed to be reciting Scripture in front of Candy, but she seemed to be listening attentively. When Mr. Barron passed out the prizes, she asked him a question about what you had to do to win something. Was this the Candy who hadn't turned in an assignment since the beginning of the school year?

Candy's mom picked her up in front of the church after Awana, and Wendell and I walked home. We were both quiet. I stared up at the dark sky dotted with stars and remembered the verses I'd recited tonight. They were from the Psalms, and they made me feel important whenever I said them.

When I look up into the night skies and see the work of your fingers—the moon and the stars you have made—I cannot understand how you can bother with mere puny man, to pay any attention to him!

I wasn't real keen on that reference to me being a puny man, but I guess if King David who wrote the psalm thought he was puny, I didn't need to worry too much. What was comforting was the thought that God cared about me, Joshua McIntire, in Grandville, Illinois. I didn't have to worry. He would do all of the worrying for me.

I guess that meant He cared about Candy, too. Now that was hard to believe.

The minute I walked onto the playground, she spotted me. I didn't have a chance.

"Hey, Josh!" she called.

What did she want? I looked around for someplace to hide, but she kept on coming.

"Hey, Josh, what's happening?"

"Hi, Candy," I said halfheartedly.

"You really believe all that stuff about God that guy was talking about last night?" she asked.

Oh, no. Where was Wendell when I needed him? He was the one who had invited her to Awana—he should be the one to answer her questions.

But it was now or never. I wouldn't be able to face Wendell or Mr. Barron if I wasn't honest. I just couldn't understand why it was so hard.

"Yeah, I do," I said. That was easy enough.

"You mean you actually think you talk to God?" she asked.

She wasn't going to be a pushover, I could see that. But I didn't back down.

"Yeah, I do," I said. "And what's more, He answers me."

"No kidding." Candy looked impressed.

I was encouraged to continue. "It takes some getting used to in the beginning," I said. "Sometimes you feel strange, but if you keep it up, pretty soon you know there's a real Person listening to all of your problems."

"Boy, and have I got some problems," Candy said.

I couldn't argue with her about that. I'd never met anybody with more.

"So maybe you can tell me more about this talking to God stuff later," Candy said. "I've got to go."

Wow, what a conversation! I couldn't believe I'd had the courage for it.

Mr. Shonkwiler was assigning teams for the Battle of the Books. That's a contest our public library sponsors every year. I really wanted to be on Wendell's team. He'd read just about every book in the library.

But I couldn't keep my mind on what Mr. Shonkwiler was saying. I kept thinking about Miss Murphy. I had my own hypothesis about why she'd stopped writing, and it wasn't to go on vacation. I was certain she was sick and couldn't get out of bed. But how could I find out?

"Team One will be Wendell, Josh, Candy, Trevor, and Sandy."

I thought I heard my name and sat up sharply in my seat. Everybody laughed.

"I'm not sure that Josh heard that, so I'll repeat it for his benefit," Mr. S. said. "Team One will be made up of Wendell, Josh, Candy, Trevor, and Sandy."

Candy looked in my direction and smiled.

Oh great. Just what we needed. Trevor and Sandy were okay, although Trevor would needs lots of extra coaching. But at least he'd work hard. Candy's idea of hard work was rearranging her bangs. There went my dream of being on the first-place team this year. Oh well. Easy come, easy go.

While Mr. S announced the rest of the teams, I let my mind wander again. If Miss Murphy was sick, why didn't she call a doctor herself? Maybe she didn't have a phone in her bedroom. Maybe she was afraid of doctors. Maybe she was just independent and didn't want to bother anybody.

By the time the dismissal bell rang, I had devised a plan to rescue Miss Murphy. She would forever be indebted to me. She would probably even write me into her will.

I flew out of my seat like a shot from a cannon, grabbed my book bag from the hook in the hall, and raced down the stairs. I couldn't wait to get to her house. Now that I'd made up my mind, there was no time to lose. As I ran, I thought briefly of asking Sonny about my idea first, but that would take too long. I had the feeling that Miss Murphy needed me now.

When I reached her house, my feeling of certainty vanished. The house looked more mysterious today, and I shivered at the thought of what I was about to do. But I just knew that Miss Murphy was in danger.

I walked up the front steps and tried the door handle. Somehow I had expected it to be open, but it didn't budge. I lifted the top of the mailbox and looked in. I recognized my letters stuffed in between the junk mail. Now what?

I walked to the back of the house. There was a screened porch, and the door was slightly ajar. I climbed the steps and walked in. My heart began to pound, but I kept on moving. I tried the door to the house, and the knob turned easily in my hand. For a split second I hesitated, thinking about what my mom would say when she found out. But the feeling that Miss Murphy needed me overruled my common sense.

I pushed through the door into the kitchen. It was a small room filled with brown and dying plants. Miss Murphy hadn't watered them for quite a while.

The next room must have been the dining room. A large rectangular table covered with a lace cloth almost filled up the room. It was all set. Miss Murphy must have been expecting a crowd. I stood in front of a china cabinet crammed with old dishes and dozens of salt and pepper shakers. Miss Murphy sure liked to collect stuff.

A sudden thud startled me, and I jumped. My heart started pounding and felt like it was going to explode. A tabby cat had leaped onto the dining room table and was staring at me with suspicious eyes. He meowed several times, hopped down, and walked toward the staircase in the living room.

It was then that I noticed the pictures. They were everywhere. Oil paintings in wild and brilliant colors. They weren't like anything I'd ever seen. I remembered that Miss

Murphy had gone to art school. Maybe she had painted them. The furniture was old-fashioned, and there were lace doilies on the arms of all of the chairs.

I couldn't put it off any longer. I had to go upstairs and see if I was right. I called Miss Murphy's name from the bottom of the stairs. There was no answer. The stairs were steep and creaky. I moved slowly, calling out her name several more times.

"Miss Murphy, are you there?"

When I reached the top step, I heard her reply. It was just a groan, but I could tell the direction. I wasn't scared anymore. I knew what I had to do. I stopped at the door to her bedroom and called her name one more time.

"Miss Murphy, it's Joshua McIntire. Are you okay?" That was kind of a stupid question. She obviously wasn't. She looked almost like a child in the big four-poster bed with a canopy.

I walked over to the side of the bed and called her name once more. "Miss Murphy, it's Joshua McIntire. I'm here to help you."

Her wispy white hair poked out from the night cap she was wearing. She opened her eyes and focused them slowly on me.

"Who are you?" she asked.

"I'm Joshua McIntire," I replied. "Your pen pal."

"My pen pal," she said. "What are you doing in my bedroom?"

"You didn't answer my letters," I said. "I got worried about you."

"I'm okay," she said. "I don't need anyone." Her eyes closed, and she didn't respond when I called her name again.

I had to find a phone fast. Miss Murphy didn't have one in her bedroom. I went back downstairs and searched under the piles of paper that were stacked everywhere. The tabby gave me several meows before vanishing again.

Her phone was an antique. I actually had to *dial* 911 instead of pushing buttons, but the result was the same.

"Grandville Emergency Services. How may I help you?"

"Please send an ambulance to 816 James Court," I said. "There's a lady here who's really sick."

"What is your telephone number, please?" the dispatcher asked.

I read Miss Murphy's number from the dial.

"And your name?"

I gave it.

"Please remain with the patient until we arrive," the voice instructed me.

When I hung up, I began to shake. Suppose the ambulance was too late and Miss Murphy died. It would be my fault for not getting here sooner. And I'd probably get arrested for breaking into her house besides.

I heard the sirens before the ambulance pulled into the driveway and hurried to the front door to let the paramedics in. "She's up here," I told them.

There were three people in the squad, and they each carried emergency equipment.

"Who is she?" the only woman of the three asked.

102

"Elizabeth M. Murphy," I replied.

"Are you a relative?" she said.

"No, I'm her pen pal," I said.

She looked at me strangely, but she didn't say anything else.

They were all working over Miss Murphy, attaching tubes and putting a mask over her face. Then they opened up the portable stretcher and lifted her from the bed.

"Is she going to be okay?" I asked.

"She's still alive," one of the men said. "We're taking her to the hospital immediately. She's very dehydrated. How long has she been sick?"

I shrugged my shoulders. "I don't know."

"Do you know of any relatives?" the woman asked.

"No," I said. "I think she's all by herself."

"Well, if she makes it, she owes you a big thank you," said the tallest of the three. "Much longer in this condition and she would have been gone."

I watched from the top of the stairs as they carefully carried Miss Murphy down. She didn't open her eyes or move at all.

When they pulled the front door shut, I sat at the top of the stairs and began to cry. Once I started I couldn't stop. I was crying for lots of things. For Miss Murphy, for not having my dad, and for being mixed up about what I'd just done. I knew better than to just walk into someone's house. But in this case, that hadn't seemed to matter.

The tabby came up the stairs and rubbed against my legs.

"Are you hungry?" I said, half sobbing the words. "Come on, let's see if there's any food around here."

There was a carton of sour milk in the refrigerator. I held my nose while I poured some into a dish. But the cat didn't seem to mind. She began lapping at once. I found some cat chow in the pantry and poured that into another dish.

All of this eating and drinking reminded me that I'd better get home. Mom would be wondering where I was. I could only imagine what her response would be to my latest adventure. My third encounter with the paramedics since moving to Grandville.

I locked the front door and left the back door the way I'd found it. Miss Murphy needed to get back in when she got better.

Mom surprised me when I told her the story.

"I think you did the right thing, Joshua," she said. "Miss Murphy's life is very important."

She called the hospital for me, and we found out that Miss Murphy was in stable condition. They were giving her food through her veins, and by tomorrow morning the doctors would know more.

I wasn't sure I'd be able to sleep after everything that had happened, but the minute my head hit the pillow I was gone.

When my alarm rang, I could think of only one thing—Miss Murphy.

"Mom, can we call the hospital again?" I begged. "I have to know how she is."

Mom found the nurse who was taking care of Miss Murphy and asked about her condition. Then she smiled and motioned for me to take the phone.

"Is this Joshua McIntire?" a voice asked.

"Yes," I said.

"This is Jeanne Lewis, Miss Murphy's nurse," she said. "I have a message for you."

"From Miss Murphy?" I said.

"Miss Murphy's doing fine and wants to see you later today."

I looked at Mom, and she was nodding. "I could come after school today," I said.

"Fine," said the nurse. "Miss Murphy will be expecting you."

I hung up the phone and looked at Mom.

"I can't wait until this afternoon," I said. "I want to go now."

"The hospital has visiting hours," Mom explained. "And you have to go to school today."

"Aw, Mom," I begged.

"Don't argue with me, Joshua," she warned. "Or I'll seriously consider grounding you for going into Miss Murphy's house without checking with a grown-up first. That was not a smart thing to do."

I hung my head. She had me there. I hustled off to my bedroom and got dressed.

Miss Murphy was going to be okay. She could still be my pen pal.

"Joshua, will life with you ever be normal?" my mom asked as she grilled French toast for me.

"I don't know, Mom," I said with a grin. "You wouldn't want to live with anyone boring, would you?"

"Every now and then the idea does appeal to me," she replied. "We've lived in Grandville for just over a year, and we seem to average an adventure a month. Just look at these gray hairs." She smiled. "If you don't stop this, I'm going to have white hair before I'm forty."

The doorbell rang. Wendell.

"Bye, Mom. See you after school," I said.

"I'm going to take off a little early today," she said. "I'll pick you up in front of school at three-fifteen, and we'll head to the hospital."

Wendell's ringing grew more persistent.

"I'm coming!" I shouted.

As I came out of the front door, Wendell didn't waste a minute.

"What's this I hear about you and Miss Murphy? How come you didn't take me along?" he demanded.

"How do you know about that already?" I asked.

"My dad was talking to one of the paramedics at the bowling alley last night," he said. "Everybody's talking about how you saved Miss Murphy's life."

"Really?" I said.

"I could have helped," he said. "You always do this fun stuff without me."

"Well, we went to Detroit together," I said. "Wasn't that

enough adventure for you? And don't forget the time you rescued me when I had my broken leg," I said. "You saved my life then."

"Yeah, I guess you're right," Wendell agreed.

Almost the whole sixth grade crowded around me when we reached the playground. Everybody's parents must have been at the bowling alley last night.

I enjoyed my celebrity status until Mr. Shonkwiler passed out the math tests we'd taken yesterday when my mind had been on Miss Murphy. There was a big red F at the top of the page, and my heart sank.

"I think this one will be a do-over," said Mr. S.

"What's a do-over?" I asked.

"It's when I throw this test out, and you do the whole thing over so you can improve your grade," he explained. "Do you think you'll be ready tomorrow?"

I nodded, grateful for the chance to try again. I had lots of people willing to give me do-overs in my life—especially God. He was always giving me another chance, just as Sonny's song said.

My mom was there at three-fifteen, and we drove to the hospital in record time. The halls were quiet, and everything smelled like medicine.

I was nervous about talking to Miss Murphy. I wondered if she'd be mad at me for coming into her house uninvited.

A nurse met us at her door. "She'd like to see Joshua alone," she said.

I looked at my mom.

"It's okay with me," she agreed. "I'll wait out here and read a magazine."

The nurse led me in. Miss Murphy was sitting up in bed. She wasn't wearing the night hat anymore, and she greeted me with a brisk hello. I could hardly believe it was the same person I'd seen yesterday.

"Well, I'm glad to meet the person who the doctors seem to think saved my life," she said. "Let me shake your hand."

She stuck out her hand, and I moved quickly across the room to take it. She was small, but her handshake was firm.

"So you're Joshua McIntire," she said. "I expected somebody taller."

I didn't know how to respond, so I mumbled, "I'm taller this year than I was last year."

"Well, no matter," she went on. "I'm no Goliath myself."

I had imagined all of the wonderful things I would say to her when we met, but my tongue was tied.

"So, tell me, what in the world possessed you to walk into my house unannounced, come into my bedroom without so much as a knock on the door, and have me carted off to this institution where they poked me full of tubes and needles?" She smiled triumphantly.

Suddenly I got my tongue back. "I didn't want to lose the best pen pal I've ever had," I said.

"Well, imagine that," she said. "An old lady like me charming a good-looking young man like you."

"I got worried when you didn't answer my letters," I explained. "And then when the mailperson told me your mail

108

was still in the box, I figured out you must be sick."

"I'm really all alone in the world, you know," she said.

"Oh no, you're not," I replied. "There are at least two people who care about you."

"Oh, really?" she said. "I suppose you're thinking of my dead brother's oldest son, who thinks he's going to inherit what's left of the money?"

"No," I said slowly. "Actually I was thinking of me and God. We both care about you."

"Nonsense," she said. "If God cared about me, why was I lying there half-dead in my bed?"

I didn't know what to say. Miss Murphy seemed to have an answer for everything. Then it came to me.

"Well, if God didn't care about you, then how come you're sitting up in bed right now talking to me?" I asked with a smug smile.

"Well, you are a bright young man, aren't you?" she said. "I'll have to keep my wits sharpened if we're going to keep company."

The nurse knocked on the door. "You can't talk much longer," she warned. "Miss Murphy needs her rest."

"Can we still be pen pals?" I asked.

"Why, of course," she said. "Although you do need to work on your inquisitive nature. But," she said with a long pause, "if you weren't so inquisitive, I wouldn't be sitting here talking to you, now would I?"

She smiled, and I smiled back.

"Good-bye, Miss Murphy," I said. "I'll be back."

◆ PARENTS ◆

Are you looking for fun ways to bring the Bible to life in the lives of your children?

Chariot Family Publishing has hundreds of books, toys, games, and videos that help teach your children the Bible and apply it to their everyday lives.

Look for these educational, inspirational, and fun products at your local Christian bookstore.